Razzle Dazzle

B.L. Blocher

Copyright © 2020 Barry Blocher

All rights reserved. No part of this book may be reproduced or transmitted in any form or by any means, electronic or mechanical, including photocopying, recording or by any information storage and retrieval system without permission in writing from the publisher.

The Emerald City Press— Southington, CT
ISBN: 978-0-578-81049-2
Library of Congress Control Number: 2020923720
Title: Razzle Dazzle
Author: B.L. Blocher
Digital distribution | 2020
Paperback | 2020

This is a work of fiction. The characters, names, incidents, places, and dialogue are products of the author's imagination, and are not to be construed as real.

Dedication

My son recently complained to me that my books are all way too inappropriate for kids his age, and just once he would actually like to read one of my books, and share it with his friends without the mortifying presence of vulgar language or violence. On his behalf, I decided to tone down the language and violence just a tiny bit. I think most would generally agree that my stories are PG-13 anyways, but this time I went the distance and brought it down a notch to a rock solid PG. I hope my son doesn't think "crap" is a swear word, or "someone getting attacked by a dog" is too violent, otherwise I'm in big trouble again! And so I wrote this epic journey which takes place deep in the Louisiana Bayou. An area rich in Cajun culture and charged with Voodoo Black Magic, Pagan rituals and some very colorful characters named Medusa, Thunder and an Army dog named Superman, just to name a few. The power of intrigue, suspense and wild imagination are locked and loaded in this incredible Cajun adventure!

And remember to beware of the Rou Gareau! It may be coming for you...

Chapter 1

The Date: October 5, 2006.
The time: 600 hours (6 AM).

As dawn broke, the steam softly drifted up off from the dew drenched grass of the operations field of Fort Chips.

An elite canine military training facility located in the south eastern region of Baton Rouge, Louisiana.

The Fort's name honored a heroic German Shepherd mix named Chips, who saved an entire US battalion during WWII.

The battalion had been hopelessly pinned down by the enemy on a Sicilian beach front.

As the US troops were under heavy attack "Chips" broke away from his handler, and raced up the beach through the heavy gunfire, dodging bullets and mortar rockets all along the way.

Chips courageously launched himself into an enemy machine gun nest and ferociously took hold of the gunner.

The other enemy soldiers in the nest were so terrified of Chips, that they immediately evacuated their position and surrendered to the US troops!

Then, later that same day while on patrol, Chips sensed danger, and alerted his handler and because of Chips keen sense of awareness, he was responsible for the capture of several more enemy soldiers.

Chips was the only animal ever awarded the Silver Star, and also received the distinguished Service Cross and a Purple Heart for his heroic deeds.

Fort Chips is commanded by Captain Jean Landry, a gritty middle aged Cajun officer, who had been in command of the esteemed canine unit that actually hunted down and captured Sadam Hussein, during Operation Red Dawn, in December of 2003 in Iraq.

He left his home in the Louisiana Bayou the day after graduating high school to pursue a career training dogs in the military, just as his father had done before him.

The army base was very active as the early morning canine training exercises for the day were about to begin.

The compound was home to approximately 100 dogs. Belgian Malinois, German Shepherds and a variety of mixed breeds.

Each was specifically trained to harvest some sort of innate ability that each particular dog was proficient at.

Their trainers and handlers were busily moving about. Some went to the obstacle and endurance courses, and some of the canines were undergoing land mine and bomb detection training, while others were doing avalanche and cadaver search training.

There was another "Elite" division of trainers on the base known as the "Terminators".

They were the specialists in charge of training canine combat behavior.

Training dogs to search out, hunt down and capture perpetrators, even kill them if commanded to.

One of the "Terminators" was Private 2nd Class Lester Duponte aka "Tunder" (Thunder).

A smug hot tempered 24 year old Cajun derelict, with a seedy past of illicit misconduct and dirty deeds, while living in the deep southern portion of the Louisiana Bayou.

He had been deployed to the training facility because of his prolific background in dog fight training and handling aggressive dogs.

It seemed handling dogs was in his blood.

Unfortunately for him, he was arrested about a year ago for illegal dog fighting, betting and disorderly conduct.

The judge gave him the option of jail time or joining the military, which the Judge felt "might just straighten him out".

In preparation for the day's K-9 take down training, Private Duponte was "suiting up" in his protective gear in the trainers locker room of the kennel.

He was accompanied by his friend, who slightly out ranked him, Private 1st class Stanislaw Kozlowski.

"Koz, why am I always da one who has to be da chew toy here? Heck, where I come from, down in de Bayou, I'm treated wid re-spect. Da fightin' dogs I trained ruled da ring. If dat Cou-yah (imbecile) Captain Landry would let me take over da training here, I'd show him how I swamp train a dog into submission, aggression and den into assasination!

I would get some re-spect and get a promotion! Maybe take over Landry's place as da head trainer!" exclaimed Private Duponte.

"This isn't your backwoods hillbilly yahoo dog fighting rooha. You're one of the lowest ranked men here on this base. Heck, even the dogs out rank you! These military K-9's are highly trained, lean, mean fighting machines! They are shipped all over the world to work side by side with our army brethren! They are fighting terrorists and enemy militias that want to destroy the United States and our allies! It's up to us to give it our all. Do you understand me, Private!" shouted Kozlowski.

"Yeah, I got it. But one day I show y'all who you're messing wid," jeered Duponte.

"Just hurry up and get going! Captain Landry is waiting on us!" shouted Kozlowski.

Reluctantly, Duponte began picking up the heavily padded dog bite protection suit pieces from a locker, and piece by piece he began attaching them onto his body.

"Dat Cou-yah recruiter promised me I would be training dogs when I signed up. Just dis week I got torn to shreds six times already! I gotta figure a way outta here and save my butt," grumbled the Private.

"Com'on, hurry up, Private! The Captain is waiting on us!" barked Kozlowski.

Duponte, feeling disrespected by Kozlowski, hesitated as if he was contemplating backing out, until Kozlowski sternly nodded him on.

He recklessly strapped on the thick bull hide padded girdle, leg, torso and abdomen protective pads.

Then a special throat collar which was designed by Lieutenant Parker, the head special tactics and design engineer of this K-9 military training complex.

The throat collar was designed to simulate the density and texture of a human throat, and it contained a special agent that consisted of a highly concentrated pheromone attractant solution specific for dogs.

It was a chemical solution that stimulated a dog's aggressive behavior when ripping and tearing at the collar, which it would then release more of the satisfying agent.

All that remained was the caged goalie helmet, his arm padding and heavily padded leather gloves.

When the private was finally outfitted, he clumsily stumbled out the door, and made his way out into the large 200 foot diamond shaped grassy chain link enclosure.

At the base of the diamonds point stood a group of soldiers, along with dog handlers positioned next to a small observation booth.

Inside the booth stood Captain Landry, who was impatiently waiting on the Private, and sternly watching with a pair of large military binoculars.

"You finally ready, Lester?" shouted Captain Landry from the release station, with an electronic megaphone.

"Laissez les bon temps roulez!" shouted the Private (a term used by Cajuns meaning "Let the good times roll!").

"Fire in the hole!" another soldier shouted.

"Get ready to let da dogs loose boys, Chey Chey!" shouted Captain Landry.

Chapter 2

Private Duponte spread his feet and braced himself as two large Belgian Malinois were aggressively tugging and lunging on their leather leashes, and their handlers were barely able to hold them back!

Then the Captain gave the order for the dogs to finally be released by their handlers.

The two dogs briskly took off, and quickly sprinted in tandem across the field toward the Private as he stood in the middle of the enclosure, bracing himself for impact!

"C'mon you Sons of Satan!!" Duponte shouted at the dogs.

Within seconds, the two dogs swiftly launched themselves onto the Private!

He was instantly knocked over, and the two vicious dogs mauled his protective suit, but they concentrated their efforts on tearing at his collar and going for his throat!

Suddenly the Private felt the protective collar slipping as the two dogs were relentlessly trying to rip through it!

He struggled to fight off the dogs, so that he could reposition and tighten his safety collar, but his heavy leather gloves and thick arm pads prevented him from accomplishing the mobility he needed to correct it!

The dogs were overly aggressive and very quick.

Then suddenly he felt the collar coming off, and he felt their hot breath and the splattering saliva of the dogs at his throat!

"Help!! Help!!!!" The Private frantically screamed, as he desperately shielded his throat with his thick arm pads.

"Stand Down!!" the Captain's voice shouted, and the handlers shouted "Halten Siesh!" (a german command to "stand down") whereupon both dogs immediately halted their attack and readily returned back to their handlers.

"You aw-right Lester?" shouted the Captain through his electronic megaphone.

"I'm trew with dis buull crap! Dis be da 7th time dis week I almost got my throat ripped apart! You can go find yourself a half looped Creol next time! I ain't doin' dis no more!!" shouted the Private as he began abruptly stripping off his protective gear, and kicking it across the enclosed field.

"What shall we do about Private Duponte, Captain Landry?" Private Kozlowski hesitantly asked.

"He'll settle down in a bit, he's a tough one. Dat's why dey call him "Tunder". He blows up, and den you count to 5 and it goes away.

Dat Cajun boy grew up in my neck of Louisiana, Acadiana. In da heart of Cajun country. We all knew of his family well. Dey be involved in some pretty bad tings. Mostly dog fightin' and moonshine in'.

Lester grew up not knowin' who his daddy was. But his Mamma, Lucille is a Voodoo Witch. She's a very powerful woman, and knows da Black Magic very well.

When she was a child her mamma's best friend and neighbor was Donorah D'Bordeau, who was herself a high level Voodoo Priestess from Haiti. She took Lucy under her wing and trained her in da art of Voodoo black magic for many years.

A few years ago, Donorah died when a hurricane blew her house down.

Somehow Lucille took in all of Donorah's magical powers, and she became the most powerful witch in da Bayou, and most anywhere for dat fact.

When I was a kid, we actually went to high school together. Lucille was madly in love wid me. She was quite a beauty too, but she was too wild and aggressive for me.

One evening she actually tried putting a Love Gris Gris on me, so I would fall in love wid her. But she wasn't powerful enough in dose days to get it done and she failed!

We had just graduated high school and I joined up in da Army. My friend Billy Fitch, heard from one of Lucy's girlfriends dat she had mixed up a Voodoo gris gris love potion, and was gonna catch it on me!

The night before I was leavin' for boot camp, me and my friends were at da swamp races and Lucille was der with her friends. We were all partyin' and havin' a good ol' time when da next thing I knew, I blacked out. I didn't know nuthin' from nuthin'! Da next morning I woke up all discombobulated and out in da woods wid a bad case of mosquito bites and poison oak!

I walked home, took a shower, and den my Pa drove me to da bus station! That was all I remembered!" exclaimed the Captain.

"The Gris Gris?" inquired Private Kozlowski.

"Voodoo, boy!" that curse-ed Black Magic will get ya, and der is no way out unless you can find a Voodoo Priest or Witch who is powerful enough to cut da spell.

But dat don't happen very often, Chey Chey. I was lucky to get away from her, or I could still be under one of her black magic spells!" stated the Captain.

"Whatever you say, Sir," replied Kozlowski as he rolled his eyes in disbelief.

"Why don't you boys take da rest of da day off, and you go with Duponte to da dawg pound, and see if you can rustle up a few simple dawgs dat we need for a Top Secret experiment dat Lieutenant Parker came up wid. We'll need about three mongrel dogs for tomorrow," stated the Captain.

The Private saluted the Captain, and then marched onto the field, toward a belligerent Private Duponte.

"Hey Duponte, get yourself together, we are going shopping at the dog pound!" shouted Kozlowski.

"Joie de vivre" he shouted back.

"What does that mean?" shouted Kozlowski.

"It's a joy to be alive! Let's get the brim stones out o' here, and maybe we will have time to swing by and get us a bucket order of Crawdads on de way back!" exclaimed the Private.

Chapter 3

Duponte quickly returned to the locker room and tossed his battered gear into a locker, and quickly put his regulation army fatigues back on.

"Aw-right, let's get it on!" exclaimed Duponte.

The two men enthusiastically left the compound, taking one of the K-9 transport vehicles, and then they drove approximately 20 miles to the New Orleans dog pound.

When they arrived at the pound, they were overwhelmed by the stench and the noise of barking dogs.

As they exited their truck, they were greeted by an employee of the kennel.

Duponte was familiar with the man.

He was an animal control officer that worked at the kennel, his name was Duffy.

Duffy was a short chubby Cajun, who barely shaved once a week, and ran yellow mayonnaise through his long black hair to keep it slicked down.

Duponte had done a lot of business with Duffy, in which he supplied the Private with fighting dogs from the kennel, and they were also related in some way, second or third cousins.

"How's your Mamma and them?" asked Duponte.

Duffy was surprised to see Duponte in military attire since he was usually dressed as a Cajun swamp person.

"Tunder! I didn't know it's Mardi Gras, why you dressed up like da Po Po?" chuckled Duffy.

"I ain't no cop, Cou-yah. You know I got busted for fighten' my dawgs! Da judge man told me;

'You got to go to Yale or da Army,' so I told da Judge, Yazoo!! Yezz, sir! I'll go to Yale! Den da judge called me a 'dumb redneck' and said; 'Jail boy! Not Yale boy!' so I joined up," chuckled Duponte.

"Dis here is my friend and partner in crime, Private 1st Class Stanley Kozlowski. He is my superior officer. Haha, where I'm only a Private 2nd class loser. You'll see, one day soon I'll be bossin' him around the base! You watch out Koz, be nice to me or I'll make sure you'll be cleanin' out da dog poop from da kennel wid a tooth pic!" Duponte joked.

Private Kozlowski was not amused and gave Duponte a sarcastic look.

"He ain't got no sense of humor. Mostly cause he's a Yankee from New York City, but don't hold dat against em'. Mais, he's a Cajun at heart since I took him under my wing," chuckled Duponte.

"Pleased to meet you," stated Kozlowski.

"Yeah sir, lets pass a good time!" Duffy cheered.

"So Duff, we need some dogs, three of em, and dey gots to be nice nice. What can ya catch for me?" stated Private Duponte.

"Follow me, Tunder," stated Duffy, and the men followed him into the large kennel.

There were dozens of rows of 4'x8' chain link enclosures. Each one was occupied by a jumping or wildly yapping dog. It was ridiculously loud and the smell was awful!

In one of the cages there was actually a huge wild boar.

"Where did you catch dat pig, man?" Duponte questioned.

"I trapped him under the west Bayou bridge! We're gonna have a Boucherie dis weekend at my Mamma's plantation house!

Maybe you boys can come, but ya gonna need a boat to get der?" Duffy proudly stated.

"Dat be a group pig roastin' party. I doubt da Captain will let us go, since he knows how Cajun's get when dey get drunk. And I'm sure der will be plenty of liquor and fightin' goin' on. I've been to your Mamma's Boucheries before. Dey always end up with somebody gettin' punched, stabbed or shot," stated Duponte.

Duffy shrugged his shoulders and nodded in agreement.

"Okay, Duffy, so catch me some mongrel dogs so we can get goin'. I'm gonna take 1st class to da 'Craw-Dad Shack' before we gotta get back to da base," stated Duponte.

"Dat's gonna be a tall order Tunder. All we mostly pick up nowadays are these mangey Pit Bulls. Dey cute when dey pups, but den dey grow up and some of dem get mean and ugly, and so dey get dumped back off here or we have to pick em up off da street. Nobody wants dem, even dough dey can be a good pet. Dey got a bad rap because of guys like you, who trained dem to fight.

So what we do is we tell da folks who come in lookin' for a pet, dey be a "Lab mix" and off dey go. Most of da time we find dem running loose again, or dey come straight back here, and sometimes dey don't. I just like to make sure der are no kids or cats in da house before I let em' go," stated Duffy.

"We just need three family friendly dogs," stated Kozlowski.

Duffy began scratching his head.

"How about a "Lab mix"? Would dat due?" he smiled.

"Just give us what you got and we'll deal wid da Captain," stated Duponte.

Duffy hastily grabbed a handful of leash ropes and quickly gathered up 3 "Lab Mixes" and carefully walked them out of the kennel and placed them into the dog compartments on the truck.

"Tanks Bon ami, see ya round!" said Duponte.

"Goodbye, Tunder. Send Millard at da Shack my Cher, Cher (Love)! Maybe I'll see you at my Mamma's, Saturday night!" replied Duffy.

Duponte shrugged his shoulders and replied;

"Maybe, Bon ami. Maybe."

Chapter 4

The two soldiers drove off with the dogs halfheartedly barking in their compartments and after traveling a short distance Duponte stopped the truck and parked next to a rundown shanty, which seemed to be a condemned diner.

It had an old faded and dilapidated hand painted wooden sign which read; "The CrawDad Shack" and it was hanging lopsidedly by a pair of rusty old wires.

"What is this dump?" questioned Kozlowski.

"Dis here hunka dump diner got da best tasten' Crawdads dis side of New Orleans! Come on, before da Captain starts lookin' for us," stated Duponte.

The two men quickly jumped out of the truck and entered the diner through an old peeling green wooden screen door, with a long self closing spring connected to the top of it.

There were hundreds of large black flies buzzing around the light bulbs that were dangling from the ceiling, and sitting against the wall was an old dusty jukebox with its colorful lights flashing, and it was playing Zydeco music. About a half dozen patrons were sitting at the counter, slurping down piles of bright red steamed crayfish.

"It smells like rotten shrimp in here!" quietly commented Kozlowski.

"Well, if it ain't GI Joe and Ken. Where have you been, Tunder? I heard you got busted for animal abuse," stated a tall slim elderly black man, who was standing behind the counter.

His name was Millard, and he was the diners owner.

He was partially bald, and had short snow white hair covered with a New Orleans Saints football hat and was chewing on a short stubby cigar.

"You heard right, Millard. Mais, now here I am goin' Awol for your crawdads, so set us up wid a bucket! I'm gonna teach dis here yankee how to pinch da tail and suck da heads off des critters!

By da way, I just saw Duffy at da pound, and he sends his Cher Cher!" stated Duponte.

Millard smiled and then left for the kitchen. When he returned he was carrying a small metal bucket filled with dozens of boiled red crayfish.

"Watch me green horn, and den dig in!" instructed Duponte.

Just as Duponte had torn the head off his first juicy crawfish, the old wooden screen door of the restaurant swung wide open, and a large black man wearing an orange blazer, and an open cuban shirt with several heavy gold chains and medallions hanging from them, entered the diner.

He was wearing a large straw panama hat, and was sweating profusely as he continuously wiped his forehead with a soaked crumbled up handkerchief.

He strutted into the restaurant, as if he was going to "bust a move" and he was dragging a young teenage black girl behind him on a dog leash, which was attached to a sharp spiked dog collar that was strapped tightly around her neck. She seemed scared and struggled as she was desperately trying to get away from him.

He yanked her along and told her to sit on the floor next to him, as he sat down at his usual reserved post seat at the end of the counter.

The restaurant owner cautiously approached the large man.

"What's going on Brud? Dat ain't cool what you doin' to that poor girl. How about you let her off da floor and take dat collar off her, and I'll feed both ya for nothin?" stated the owner.

"What you talkin' about man?! This here is my new puppy and a puppy belongs on the end of my leash. Now set me up with a bucket, and I'll drop a few on the floor for my dawg," replied Brud.

Private Kozlowski became visibly upset as he glanced around the restaurant, and saw that no one was going to come to the aid of this young girl, and they just continued on eating as if nothing was wrong.

Kozlowski heroically began to get up out of his stool to confront the large man, but Duponte caught him and told him to stand down.

"I'll take care of it, Koz. Dis scum is a really bad dude. I know him," stated Duponte.

Duponte slowly moved away from his seat and cautiously approached the man, who was now tearing apart his meal.

"How's ya mamma and them, Brud?" stated Duponte.

Brud glanced over his shoulder and noticed Duponte approaching him.

His mouth was full of crayfish, and there were bits of meat stuck all over his wet lips, and the juice was dripping from the corners of his mouth as he gorged on his meal.

"Yo! Stop your shiny white butt right there, Duponte! You ain't got one of those crazy fightin' dogs with you, do you?!" Brud exclaimed, as his gluttonously chewed food sprayed from his mouth.

He instantly pulled out a large caliber chrome pistol from a holster concealed inside his Blazer jacket, and he nervously scanned the area around him, eying for one of Duponte's vicious dogs.

"Naw, I had to give up on da fighten' dogs. I got busted one too many times and dey made me join up. Now, I'm a dawg toy for da army," replied Duponte.

"Do you owe me money or do you want to give me some money? Otherwise turn your milk knees around and go away," he smuggly stated.

"Mais, if it's all the same to you, I'd like to take dat young girl off your hands and let her go home. How much would that run me, Brud?" stated Duponte.

"So you're in the Army, and now you want to be Mr. Good bar? Give me 10 large and she's all yours!" Brud laughed.

"Come on Brud, she's just a kid. Let me take her back to her family!" Duponte pleaded.

"Get lost Cou-yon, before I put a nugget between your eyeballs. You ruinin' my lunch!" Brud angrily stated, and he pointed his gun at him and motioned him to back away.

Duponte knew better than to mess with Brud, for he knew that he would not hesitate killing him, and no one in the diner would "see anything".

Duponte backed away, and he motioned to his friend that they had better leave before Brud started shooting.

"What about the Crawdads?" stated Millard.

"Give em' to the girl Millard, and Duponte threw a ten dollar bill on the counter and they quickly left.

"We should call the cops on that guy," Kozlowski angrily stated as they entered the truck.

"The Po Po won't touch him. He's mixed up with some pretty bad dudes. Some are cops. Let's just get dese dogs back to da Fort before dey dehydrate," replied Duponte.

Chapter 5

The following morning Private Duponte and Private 1st Class Kozlowski reported to Captain Landry that they had acquired several dogs, and that they were in the kennel.

As the Captain listened, he opened up his desk drawer and removed a short black comb, and began combing his hair while staring into a small hand mirror, as the two men reported to him.

Partially listening as he was obsessively aligning the part in his hair.

"Good work, now y'all dismissed, and Lester, be on da field at 1300 hours (1:00 PM), suited up. Lieutenant Parker arranged some kinda 'Top Secret' experiment and he stated dat he wants you, Private 2nd Class Duponte on da field," ordered the Captain.

Duponte exhaled a heavy grieving breath, and a look of disgust at the thought of suiting up again, but reluctantly he agreed.

The men saluted Captain Landry and then left the room.

"While you are waiting around Duponte, get a bucket and mop, and wash the floor in the Captain's office. I noticed it's covered with mud and dog excrement," ordered Kozlowski.

"Why is every crappy job around here on me?!" exclaimed Private Duponte.

"Someday you will get to be ordering around someone under your rank, but until then, go get the mop and bucket!" ordered Private Kozlowski.

A few minutes later Duponte returned to the Captain's office and knocked on his door.

"Who dat!" the Captain shouted.

"It's Private Duponte, Sir. Request permission to come in and mop da dog crap off your floor, Sir," stated the Private.

"Okay, come on in. Mais, make it quick. Lieutenant Parker is on his way over here and we need to speak privately," stated the Captain.

The Private quickly began mopping the floor, and after several minutes there was a soft knock on the Captain's door.

"Com on in, da doors open," the Captain shouted.

Lieutenant Parker entered his office carrying a stainless steel Attache' case and placed it onto Landry's desk.

"You gonna have to go now, Private," ordered Captain Landry.

The Lieutenant avoided making eye contact with Duponte, and seemed uncomfortable as Duponte gathered his bucket of filthy water and wet mop, and left the officers to themselves.

The Captain closed the door behind him, and locked it.

Duponte, being a curious Cajun, remained outside the Captain's door and placed his ear against it, eavesdropping on their conversation.

"Good Morning Captain Landry. I've completed my testing and I believe we are ready to test the "Tiger Shark" on a canine test subject this afternoon," stated Lieutenant Parker.

"Good, yesterday I sent da boys out to da pound to pick up a few mongrel dawgs for today's experiment. Why don't you sit down, and explain how dis ting is gonna work," inquired Captain Landry.

Lieutenant Parker pulled up a chair and sat down as he opened the metal Attache' case.

The inside of the case was made of soft gray foam, and there were approximately 50 jelly bean sized metallic capsules pressed into the foam cutouts in the case.

There were also two small black transmitters and several small pump spray vials of a clear solution also set in their own foam cutouts.

Captain Landry surveyed the contents and was baffled at the objects.

"So, what have you got here? All I see is a case full of jambalaya," stated the Captain Landry.

"I've created a cutting edge miniscule undetectable device, that when implanted into the ear canal of a canine, it can remain dormant until it is activated by either of these transmitter devices. Where apon once activated, the implanted "Bean" stimulates the neurotransmitters and hormonal secretion glands of the canines brain which prompts the release of UBE2V2 and ZNF227, which then in turn reacts with the animals hypothalamus and cerebral cortex of its brain to induce vicious aggressive behavior," stated Lieutenant Parker.

"Would ya please run dat by me in Cajun, so I can understand what da crawdad you are talkin' about!" exclaimed Captain Landry.

"Sorry, Captain. These tiny beans are actually an electronic stimulator which acts as a catalyst that reacts with certain parts of a dog's brain.

The parts which are responsible for aggressive behavior.

It will work on any sized canine.

When I push the green button on this transmitter, the implanted device activates, and the animal's brain begins to produce a heap load of "Crush, Kill, Destroy juice!".

To turn it off, all you have to do is press the red button on the transmitter.

It instantly cuts out, and after about 10 seconds the dog returns back to normal.

Each "Bean" only works once. After a few hours it passes down through the animal's eustachian tube and into the animal's throat, and it gets harmlessly swallowed. You just have to make sure the canine stays in range, though.

Otherwise the only way to stop it is to dispatch the animal," stated the Lieutenant.

"What are da spray bottles for?" inquired Landry.

"Captain, have you ever heard of a mad dog racing into a crowd and singling out one particular person, and then viciously attacking them over all the others?

A dog's sense of smell as you know, is about 100,000 times more powerful than humans.

A canine can detect one single grain of sugar in 1000 grains of salt.

On a good day where there is no wind or weather issues, and a low density of objects such as buildings and forest, a dog can easily detect a scent miles away.

The dog's Jacobson's organ, which is located at the base of its nostrils is responsible for picking up scents, especially pheromonal scents.

These scents usually get the animal all geared up to mate, especially if there is a female in heat in the area.

Dogs will show up from everywhere, even miles away if the scent carries.

There are other scents that can make a dog aggressive, especially if it smells food or a mate and wants to protect it.

If the dog's attention is on task, you'll then notice the "Flehmen reaction" engaging, where the animal curls its upper lip to allow more air flow to the Jacobson's organ.

When you see that, you know the animal is on to something it wants to react with.

There are specific pheromones that are odorless to humans but animals like dogs can quickly sense.

For unknown reasons, this may be why a given canine might skip over certain individuals, only to target a specific victim.

They don't like the way they smell.

The spray is a targeting mechanism for the canine to hone in on a given target.

Whatever I spray this attractant on, and it only takes a little bit, the canine will single out that entity, and lock on to it. Similarly to the experimental collar Private Duponte was wearing yesterday in the field test," stated Lieutenant Parker.

Duponte continued eavesdropping outside the Captain's door, and couldn't believe what he was hearing.

"Dat gizmo would give me a big advantage wid my fightin' dawg string back home," he thought.

Suddenly he heard footsteps coming his way, and Private Kozlowski entered the building.

Duponte quickly left the Captain's door and returned the mop and bucket to the supply room.

"You all done here?" questioned Kozlowski.

"Cu c'est bon," replied Duponte… "All is good!"

Chapter 6

It was now 1300 hours (1:00 PM) and Kozlowski had just met up with Private Duponte in the kennel locker room. Duponte was already getting prepared and strapping his protective gear on.

"What's up, Duponte? Usually you'd be cry-babying right about now about being the squeaky toy of the day? Are you feeling alright?" questioned Kozlowski.

"I'm aw-right, and full of Cher!" stated the Private.

He was excited to test the top secret device that he had overheard the Captain and Lieutenant discussing privately.

Captain Landry had hastily entered the locker room after inspecting the mongrel dogs the two men had acquired the day before.

"I thought I told you two Cou-yahs to pick up some passive dawgs. You brought back a pack of Pit bulls!" shouted the Captain.

"Well sir, it was slim pickings over there at the pound. Those family dogs get adopted pretty quickly. But the animal control officer assured us these were "Lab Mixes," nervously replied Private Kozlowski as he angrily eyeballed Duponte.

"Lab mixes?! Are you dat stupid?!! Well, dey will have to do for today. Lieutenant Parker ain't gonna be happy when I tell em' you messed up wid da dogs, Private Kozlowski!" scolded Captain Landry.

Duponte just smiled and shrugged his shoulders as Kozlowski was being reprimanded.

"By da way, Lester. Da Lieutenant must really like you. He requested you again, he said to make sure 'Private Lester Duponte' will be in da suit today," stated the Captain.

The Captain then raised a bottle of the pheromone spray, which Lieutenant Parker developed as the attractant for his experiment, and carefully gave a single spritz of the solution on Private Duponte's chest area, avoiding getting any of the vapor or mist on himself or Kozlowski.

Kozlowski and Duponte were perplexed by the spray and the Captain just mentioned it was 'Bug repellent' and then left the room.

However, based on what Duponte had overheard in the Captain's office, Duponte knew exactly what it was.

The Tiger Shark attractant.

Private Kozlowski gave Duponte a stern and angry look.

"We never should have taken those Pit bulls!" declared Kozlowski.

"Heck, you could have said "No" to Duffy too. But why do you suppose da Lieutenant is so hot for me to be da one in da dummy suit today?" questioned Duponte as he continued suiting up.

"Captain said he likes you, aren't you lucky," replied Private Kozlowski.

Chapter 7

Captain Landry returned to the kennel, and chose the most reclusive and timid "Lab mix" from the group.

It was a small brindle male that relentlessly avoided being caught.

He was hardly leash trained, and Captain Landry ultimately dragged it back to his office where Lieutenant Parker was waiting with his Attache' case.

Landry handed the small spray bottle of attractant back to him and he placed it back into its foam slot in the case.

"I sprayed it like you said, on da Privates chest," reported Landry.

"Where's the passive dog I requested?" the Lieutenant inquired.

"Da boys I sent out reported dis is all dey had at da pound. It will have to do," replied the Captain.

"That's alright, a Pit bull will do perfectly for my experiment today," he maniacally stated.

Lieutenant Parker removed one of the bean sized capsules from his Attache' case, and inserted it down into the dog's ear canal.

Pushing it deeply down into the cavity with his finger.

"Dat's it?" questioned Captain Landry.

"Just like that," replied Lieutenant Parker.

They then dragged the reluctant dog over to the training field, where Private Duponte was already waiting and dressed in his protective gear, about 100 yards out in the field.

There were several armed soldiers with long range rifles, and others with tranquilizer guns, strategically positioned all around the diamond shaped enclosure, keeping their weapons trained on the dog at all times.

Private Kozlowski greeted the Captain and the Lieutenant, then took the reluctant dog as they took their places in the observation booth.

"You ready, Duponte?!" shouted Private Kozlowski.

"Laissez les bon temps roulez'!" shouted the private.

Private Kozlowski tightly held the rope leash, and waited for the Captain's orders to release the dog.

"Fire in the hole!" shouted a soldier who was videotaping the event.

Lieutenant Parker removed the small transmitter from his shirt pocket and then pressed the green activation button.

Everyone stood silently, watching the cowering dog as he had just peed a puddle beneath himself.

"Nothings happening," whispered Captain Landry.

"It takes a minute for the levels to build up," replied Lieutenant Parker.

After a few more seconds the dog seemed agitated and rose up onto his feet, and began gently sniffing the air around him. He was becoming more and more agitated, and began focusing his attention on the air, and locating the pheromonal scent which was wafting off of Private Duponte, 100 yards away.

The dogs upper lip began to curl up, signifying the Flehmen reaction was engaging.

His brindle hair began to rise off his back and he began to growl, and then he began barking and snapping his massive teeth!

"Captain, I'm concerned! I'm not wearing a suit and this canine is becoming extremely aggressive!" shouted Private Kozlowski.

"He shouldn't bother you," replied the Lieutenant.

"SHOULDN'T?!!" Kozlowski fearfully replied.

Suddenly the dog viciously lunged toward Duponte, tearing the leash from Kozlowski's hands.

He raced across the field directing his full rage and ferocity at Private Duponte!

"Com'on you crazy Rou Garou!" Duponte shouted at the animal, as the dog manically closed in on him.

Duponte braced himself as the ferocious dog lunged up at him with his teeth fully exposed and drooling with hot slimy saliva!

In mid air the animal instinctively took hold of Duponte's leather throat guard, and then twisted its body, flipping Duponte violently down onto the ground.

The dog then began viciously mauling his protective suit, searching for an opening or weakness that it could take advantage of!

The dog became so strong and savage that he was actually beginning to tear apart Dupontes protective suit!

Duponte suddenly felt his protective collar coming apart, and began screaming for his life!

"Help!! Help!! Da Rou Garou, da Rou Garou!" shrieked the private.

It was clear that the Lieutenants implant was a success, and all that was left was to halt the attack.

"Shut him down Lieutenant," calmly stated Captain Landry.

However, Lieutenant Parker appeared to be in a trance-like state and was seemingly enjoying the fruits of his labor.

He ignored Landry's request to turn off the dog!

Once again Captain Landry aggressively ordered Lieutenant Parker to shut down the dog!

But he refused, and continued on ignoring Captain Landry's order to halt the attack!

"Dat dog is gonna kill dat boy! Shut it down!! Dat's an Order!!" shouted the Captain.

But Parker just stood there smiling in his maniacal daze, taking pleasure watching Duponte being mauled to death.

The Captain then quickly ordered a soldier to radio the snipers to tranquilize the dog.

Instantly two darts flew out and hit the dog's rump, but it had no effect on the crazed animal!

The dog was focused and ripping the protective collar to pieces!

Duponte was desperately trying to get to his feet, and run away! But the dog was supercharged and he never had a chance!

Duponte was frantically clutching his protective throat collar, trying to keep it together to protect his neck and throat from the dog's vicious attack!

But the dog was crazed and relentless, and in some sort of hellacious state of mind as he viciously and vehemently mauled the Private!!

"Take the dawg out!!" shouted Captain Landry.

A soldier instantly ordered the snipers to dispatch the out of control canine.

Instantly 4 bullets struck the dog, but like the tranquilizer darts, the bullets had no effect on him.

He was filled with so much adrenalyn that he continued attacking the Private and it seemed that he was unstoppable!

"Hit em' again!!" the Captain ordered.

Another 4 shots rang out, but this time the dog fell over and dropped to the ground!

Private Duponte continued rolling around on the ground in a fetal position, shaking and covered in his and the dogs blood.

A squad of medics raced out to treat him, and fortunately for him, the dog was finally killed in the nick of time.

The protective throat guard had just broken off, and its straps seemed to have been previously tampered with and cleanly cut through with a knife.

They helped Duponte to his feet, and he was obviously shaken and in shock!

His wrists and arms were bloodied from fending off the crazed dog, but he was lucky to still be alive.

The medics carried him back to the infirmary on a stretcher where his wounds were treated, and he was allowed to stay and rest.

He was mentally in a bad way and he continued mumbling insanely... "Da Rou Garou is coming for you! Da Rou Garou is coming for you," and he continued to just lay on his cott, dazed and in a state of shock, just staring up at the ceiling, and he kept repeating... "Da Rou Garou is coming for you...."

Chapter 8

Captain Landry turned to Lieutenant Parker and angrily punched him in the face and knocked him to the ground!!

"Da Colonel is gonna hear about dis! In da meanwhile, I'll take charge of dat Attache' case with the Tiger Shark kit," exclaimed Captain Landry.

Lieutenant Parker slowly got himself up, holding his hand over his painfully bruised cheek, as Captain Landry left with the Attache' case.

"We'll see about that Landry," he mumbled as he watched the Captain leave with his invention.

Private Kozlowski was waiting outside of Captain Landry's office when he returned with the Attache' case.

"How's Duponte?" the Captain questioned with concern.

"His wrists and arms are chewed up pretty badly, and he is shaken up, but he'll live. I doubt we'll ever get him back in the field again though," replied Kozlowski.

The Captain was relieved that Duponte was going to be alright, and he placed the Attache' case into a cabinet near his desk and locked it closed with a key.

"Sir, if I could bother you for a moment, Private Duponte was shouting "The Rou Garou?" What did that mean, Sir? I assumed it was Cajun French?" questioned the Private.

"Da legend of da Rou Garou comes from deep down in da swamps of da Bayou.

It's a vicious creature dat lives in da woods! A big ferocious Werewolf!! Hairy and scary!

It walks on two feet, like a man and is stronger dan a grizzly bear!

He got a big wolf head wid giant fang teeth and pointy ears! It likes to eat human flesh, but will sometimes just kill ya and drink up all your blood.

It'll sneak up on you when you don't expect it, and den get ya wid its giant finger claws and drag you away and feast on your body!

Pray boy, dat it eats you all up! If it don't, you will become one too! Some have sworn to see a Rou Garou dat was disfigured, like big chunks missin' from deir bodies, and some crawlin' around wid no legs in the deep woods of da Bayou. Dose are da unlucky ones dat didn't get eaten all da way!" exclaimed the Captain.

The Private shook his head, and didn't seem to believe that such a creature did actually exist.

"Sir, Duponte and I overheard the medics talking about Lieutenant Parker, and how he refused to call off the dog.

They believe he was trying to kill Private Duponte, Sir," stated Private Kozlowski.

"Between you and me Private, I do believe he wanted to watch that dog murder Duponte. I'm writin' up a report to send to the Colonel. I don't care how smart and important da Lieutenant is, that poor boy almost died out dere because of him," replied Captain Landry.

"If it's alright with you, I'd like to go check on Private Duponte. Do you think that maybe he could get some sort of promotion or purple heart? Something to lift his spirits? I think that would make him feel better," stated the Private.

"I'll see what I can come up wid. Go ahead, you are dismissed," replied the Captain.

The Private saluted, and then left the building, and made his way back to the infirmary, where Duponte was still recovering on his cott.

His wrists and arms were bandaged and there was an ice pack on his shoulder.

"Looks like you might get something out of this," stated Kozlowski.

"What da chili peppers was that dog on! I've never seen nothin' like dat before!" commented Duponte.

"It looks like Lieutenant Parker is going to go down for letting that dog maul you. The Captain told him several times to shut the dog down. He had some sort of Top Secret radio transmitter in his pocket, but Parker refused to do it!

He wanted to see that dog kill you, Lester!" stated Kozlowski.

"I don't get it, I never did nothin' to him. Why would he want me dead?" questioned Duponte.

"I don't think it was about you. I think that in his crooked mind, for his experiment to be a success, someone had to die," stated Kozlowski.

"But somebody cut da straps on da collar. Who else could of done dat?" stated Duponte.

"I guess that dog must have had a knife in his pocket," chuckled Kozlowski.

"Koz, I've got to tell you somethin'. After I cleaned the Captain's office dis mornin', da Lieutenant showed up wid dat metal Attache' case.

Da Captain kicked me out of da room, but I listened through da door.

Inside da case was a device dat da Lieutenant invented. It makes a passive dog go aggressive and viciously attack.

I heard him explain to da Captain about a Bean dat he put into da dogs ear canal.

Den a special targeting spray placed on da victim, and den push da button on da transmitter, and da dog will zero in on it's target and go ballistic on dat person! Dat's what da experiment was about today.

Da Captain put da spray on me, and when it came time, da Lieutenant pushed the Bean into da dogs ear and pushed da transmitter button when dey were at da observation booth!" exclaimed Duponte.

"That sounds pretty far-fetched that there is a secret device that turns a dog into a raging killer. But, I did see the Lieutenant holding something that did look like a transmitter.

Just get some rest and we could talk about it more in the morning," stated Kozlowski.

After the brief visit, Private Kozlowski then left and retired to his barracks for the evening.

Duponte continued lying on the cott, reliving the horrendous attack that he narrowly escaped that afternoon.

"Somethin' stinks around here, and I'm gonna get to da bottom of it.

But one thing for sure, Lieutenant Parker wanted me dead and I'm gonna find out why," he whispered to himself.

Chapter 9

It was approximately 0100 hours (1 AM) the following morning when Lieutenant Parker clumsily staggered into his laboratory, searching for more liquor to add to his already drunken stupor.

He was extremely upset over Captain Landry's threat to report him to the Colonel, and that his prized creation was confiscated and locked up in the Captain's office.

Unbeknown to the Captain and the others at the base, the Lieutenant had incurred a very large gambling debt with a local thug named Beauregard J. Bobbit, aka Bobo.

Bobo was a heavy set middle aged sloppy Creol from the swamps of southern Louisiana.

He spoke softly and slowly, giving the impression that he was a reasonable and educated gentleman, but he was anything but that.

In fact when it came to money, he was a sleazy, greedy racketeer.

He regularly wore a stained and wrinkled white seersucker suit, along with a flat top straw boater hat and black and white patent leather wing tipped shoes.

He also carried a walking stick which doubled as a concealed sword, along with a snub-nosed 38 special revolver hidden in his waistband.

He was involved in a variety of illegal businesses ranging from small-time bookmaking, gambling and loan sharking to dog and chicken fighting.

Anything against the law, all the way down the book of illicit ways to make money, Bobo was involved with.

Unfortunately for Lieutenant Parker, about two years prior he was lured into a street gambling game called "Razzle Dazzle" during Mardi Gras, by one of Bobo's seductive cronies.

He had just arrived at Fort Chips, and was exploring the city of New Orleans and the Carnival for the first time, during a weekend leave from the base.

He was wandering the busy streets of the French quarter which was inundated by dozens of illegal gambling carnival booths, when suddenly a mystical young black woman caught his attention.

She had dozens of multi colored dreadlocks stemming from her head with dried striking rattlesnake heads attached to each of the ends, and a thick brightly colored Rattlesnake tattoo which was imprinted on her skin.

The snake's tail rattlers began on the back of her left hand, and the tattoo continued up and wrapped itself around her arm all the way up to her shoulder.

Then it continued and wrapped itself around her neck, and over to her opposite shoulder, and it continued wrapping itself down her other arm, and the terrifying head of the snake with its gaping venomous fangs, appeared to be viciously striking and ended on the back of her right hand.

If that wasn't enough, she wore green lizard-like lenses in her eyes, and she was wearing several pagen rings and bracelets on her hands and wrists.

Dangling from her ears were a pair of dried rooster feet twined with assorted birds feathers and long dangling colorful ribbons.

She saw that she had captured the Lieutenant's eye, and she instantly began her pitch of seductively enticing the Lieutenant, as she lured him into her gaming lair.

All for the opportunity to win a brand new 75" flat screen TV, valued at over $5,000 and to take all of his money.

"Hey Sergeant Slaughter, please come on over and play my Razzle Dazzle game, and take this TV off my hands so I can finally go home! This is the last of the big boy's that I have left!

But don't you check the serial number! My boss acquired a truck load of these big screens, and they were all stolen from a Walmart big rig!

My boss would be happy just to get a few bucks for them, since they were stolen merchandise, and they didn't cost him a penny," she teased.

The bait was dangling right in front of the Lieutenant's salivating mouth, and he couldn't resist winning that big flat screen TV.

"What's your name beautiful?" the Lieutenant asked.

"Meduusaaa, I am the Guardian Protectress!" she slithered.

"Ok, Medusa, I'm not going to look you in the eyes, but I do need a TV, and the guys at the base will sure be impressed when I carry that big screen back into the barracks!

What's this Razzle Dazzle game about and how do I win?" inquired the Lieutenant.

"Razzle Dazzle is a game of skill, where all you have to do is pay me $20 to toss these 8 marbles into the tray of these numbered holes. You progressively add the numbers up to the strike goal amount of 40. When you do, this big TV is yours, and I can finally go home!

Maybe you will come with me?" she lustfully stated and winked.

"A brand new flat screen for 20 bucks?!

This is going to be like taking a biscuit from a puppy!" the Lieutenant thought.

Razzle Dazzle was a simple game which preyed on suckers and tourists.

The locals all knew all about this scam.

By throwing the marbles the player wins points by adding up the random numbers they landed on to achieve a strike goal (Usually 40 points) which seems easy, but is almost impossible to do.

Medusa continued flirting with the Lieutenant and he couldn't resist.

The Lieutenant was seemingly taken aback by her advances, but eagerly paid the macabre woman $20, and to his amazement, right off the bat, on the Lieutenants first few rolls, Medusa jubilantly explained that his numbers added up to over half of the strike goal of 40!

"3+1+5+5+3=29" Medusa exuberantly stated.

The Lieutennant quickly noticed that she had added incorrectly in his favor, and beleived this was going to be easy since she was "a dumb street person".

Unfortunately for the Lieutenant this was part of her scheme to draw him into the game.

"You're more than half way to that flat screen on your first few tosses, Sarg!" egged on Medusa.

The Lieutenant quickly began throwing more and more money at her as he was constantly in reach of that TV, but always fell just a bit short, and had to pay up and try again and again.

He was psychologically sucked into the game, and he just kept throwing more and more of his money at Medusa until he had nothing left.

The Lieutenant believed that he was too far in to stop, without winning that big TV.

Then Medusa began offering credit to the Lieutenant, double or nothings' and even threw in more prizes to keep the Lieutenant from leaving, and so he continued on playing.

After every turn he believed that his luck would soon change, and that he would win back all his money and win the TV.

In the beginning it seemed all the Lieutenant had to do was throw the marbles and add up the numbers, and when he achieved 40 points the TV was his.

"This was going to be easy! How could I lose against this dumb carnival girl who can't even add simple numbers?" he thought.

Unfortunately for the naive' Lieutenant, he was suckered into the scam, and within an hour he had already lost over $10,000!

A ridiculous amount, but he desperately believed that any minute his luck was bound to change, and it would return to him on every "next throw" as he hoped he would recoup his losses, and still win that TV.

But the way the game was rigged it was mathematically impossible for the Lieutenant to win anything.

Desperately, the Lieutenant pleaded with Medusa to forgive his debt since he was in the military and new to the area, but the sleazy woman became aggressive and demanded the money!

She then called in a pair of "Leg breakers" to "rough up" the Lieutenant, and she demanded that he cough up the money or else they would break his legs to start, and if he still didn't come up with the money she would put a Voodoo Gris Gris on him!!

With no other means of income and no savings, the Lieutenant was then encouraged by the thugs to join into more gambling activities, where he could possibly win enough money to wipe his debt clean with Bobo, or else bad things were going to happen to him and his family.

This time the Lieutenant was pressured into a game of 3 Card Monte, and it was all over for him.

Medusa let him win a few hands at the beginning but immediately upped the stakes, burying the Lieutenant into a deeper hole.

His previous debt had more than doubled to over $21,000! He was suckered into a gambling debt that there was no way he could pay off, and if he didn't make his payments (with interest), Bobo's henchmen would certainly cause him harm, if not his life.

Now he was in deep debt, and under Bobo's wicked thumb.

Bobo also knew Private Duponte and had a toxic relationship with him.

They were both from the same area of the Bayou, and both competed against each other with their own illegal activities.

However, Bobo had a grudge to settle with Duponte over a bad bet, and was angry because he claimed that Duponte had cheated him out of a $65,000 purse in a crooked dog fight.

Apparently Bobo's dog had brutally defeated Duponte's dog. The dog was virtually down and out, beaten and lying in the center of the ring.

But just before the fight was called in Bobo's favor, Duponte's dog miraculously got up, and with a second wind, he leaped onto the back of Bobo's dog, and with a decisive bite, wound up winning the fight!

Bobo claimed Duponte's dog was drugged and the fight was fixed, but Duponte didn't see it that way and so began the feud.

Fearing black magic retribution from Duponte's Voodoo Witch mother Lucille, Bobo kept his distance from Duponte. But when he discovered that Duponte was now enlisted at the same facility as Lieutenant Parker, he bided his time and made an arrangement with Lieutenant Parker that would wipe his gambling debt clean.

All he had to do was arrange an accident to kill Duponte.

"Now that I had failed and Duponte was still alive, Bobo and his gang will certainly be coming for me! They'll want to shut me up, and prevent me from talking forever!" feared Lieutenant Parker.

If word ever got out to the police, or even worse to Lucille that Bobo had put a hit on her son, Bobo's life was over.

He would most likely succumb to some sort of wicked black magic hex or be cursed for the rest of his life, compliments of Lucille.

In dire desperation, to save his own life and wipe his debt clean with Bobo, the Lieutenant had no choice but to sneak into the infirmary and finish Duponte off as he slept.

The Lieutenant removed his jacket and put on his long white lab coat which was hanging next to the door on a metal hook, just as he had done out of habit every time he entered his Lab.

As he drunkenly staggered toward his desk, he didn't notice the fresh wet circular stain on the back of his lab coat.

He stumbled his way over to his desk and he recklessly plunged down into his squeaky rolling chair, and frantically began rifling through his desk drawers, until he found exactly what he was looking for.

A large syringe full of Telazol, a lethal and potent dog euthanizing drug that was kept on hand in case of an emergency.

"I'll sneak into the infirmary and inject this into Duponte's neck, and he'll never wake up!" the Lieutenant maniacally thought to himself.

Suddenly the lights in the Lab flicked off, and the Lieutenant heard the laboratory door quickly open, then close.

The Lieutenant became alarmed and panicked!

He believed Bobo's gang was there and coming for him!

"Who's there?!! Bobo! Is that you?!!" the Lieutenant exclaimed.

But there was only silence.

Strangely, he thought he heard the wheezing "panting" of a large animal in his laboratory.

"Ha huh, Ha huh, Ha huh, Ha huh, Ha huh…." the panting continued.

"I must be losing my mind, and I'm hearing things!" he exclaimed to himself in his drunken state.

"It wasn't my fault Bobo! I cut the straps on Duponte's collar, and did everything I could to let the dog finish him off! But Landry stepped in and stopped it!

I'm going over to the infirmary right now to finish off Duponte with this syringe full of dog killer!" he anxiously declared.

But there was no response.

Only the panting sound which continued growing louder!

"You cheated me in that game of Razzle Dazzle Bobo, and I had no way out of my debt to you! Because you were afraid of Dupontes mother, you dragged me into this mess to do your dirty work!" shouted the Lieutenant.

And then the Lieutenant seemed to hear a faint deep voice echoing from somewhere in the room, as the "panting" continued to get slightly louder!

"Ha huh, Ha huh, Ha huh, Ha huh…"

"Da Rou Garou is a comin' fo yooou..." a voice faintly whispered.

"Ha huh, Ha huh, Ha huh, Ha huh…"

"Da Rou Garou is a comin' fo yooou,...over and over it repeated, and louder and louder it became!"

"Lieutenant Parker in a desperate panicked state, frantically raced towards the Laboratory door to escape! Knocking over much of his lab equipment that was in his path!

When suddenly one of the other "Lab mixes" that Private's Duponte and Kozlowski had acquired at the pound days before, pounced out of darkness, and blocked the Lieutenant's only path of escape!

The muscular dog began to softly growl, and focused his blue eyed stare as the Lieutenant slowly began backing away from the beast.

The dog's demeanor was rapidly changing as it was becoming more and more aggressive!

His growling escalated, and saliva began pouring from his mouth as the animal bared his massive sharp teeth!

The dog began curling his upper lip, and drew more air into his nasal passages, while continuing to target the Lieutenant as his prey.

Lieutenant Parker instantly realized that this dog was under the influence of the Tiger Shark, and that he was the object of his aggression.

He had no choice but to make a run for the supply closet, but the dog was much faster and was ferociously enraged!

He leapt at the Lieutenant, grabbing him by the back of his arm and violently jerked him to the ground, where he then began viciously mauling the Lieutenant!

The Lieutenant was desperately trying to fight off the dog! He was hopelessly trying to protect his own throat, while at the same time trying to inject the dog with the syringe full of Telazol that he had intended on using on Duponte!

But the dog was too strong, and it's blood was pumping full of red raging madness!

In a final act of desperation, the Lieutenant took a chance and grabbed a hold of the dog's leather collar, and aimlessly thrusted the syringe into the dog's massive neck!

But in doing so he left his own throat exposed and completely vulnerable!

The vicious dog seized on the opportunity and latched on! With his last breath the Lieutenant shrieked, but unfortunately it was too late, as he was unable to push down the syringes plunger, and inject the euthanizing drug into the vicious beast.

Then, it was ultimately over for the Lieutenant and he was dead.

In an instant the dog's demeanor flipped, and he ceased his vicious attack, and backed away from the Lieutenant's lifeless bloody body.

The syringe still full of the euthanizing drug fell out of his neck and onto the floor.

He calmly licked his chops, and once again became passive.

The laboratory door once again mysteriously opened, and the dog happily pranced out of the laboratory with his tail wagging, and then the door closed again.

Chapter 10

The following morning at 0557 (5:57 AM) the Fort's emergency sirens began sounding off! Military police raced towards the Lieutenants laboratory, and an ambulance was called in.

One of the Lieutenant's assistants had just arrived at the lab, and she discovered the Lieutenant's completely mutilated body.

It was a heinous sight, and she barely staggered out of the lab before passing out in the arms of a soldier.

Earlier that morning, one of the base's military police officers spotted the blood drenched dog that perpetrated the violent attack.

However, it slipped away as it dashed through the main gate of the base, and then disappeared into the adjacent woods prior to the discovery of Lieutenant Parker's body.

Private Kozlowski rushed to report to the Captain who was on his way to the scene.

"Sir! Lieutenant Parker was just found dead in his lab, mauled to death! And Private Duponte is gone! He is not in the infirmary! He's missing along with "Superman" (the company's 5 star German Shepard)!" exclaimed Private Kozlowski.

The Captain became distraught and reversed his path. Instead of going to Lieutenant Parker's Laboratory, he headed toward his own office.

When he arrived there, he was in a panicked state, and he immediately noticed that the locked cabinet which contained the Attache' case with the Tiger Shark was broken into, and it was gone!

"Call da Po-lice, da CIA and da FBI!" frantically ordered the Captain.

"Duponte is Awol and he just stole possibly da most insidious weapon known to man since da gun!" shouted the Captain.

The Private rushed out of his office and down a short hallway where there was a phone hanging on the wall, and he began contacting the local Police, the FBI and the CIA.

The Captain recklessly plunged himself down into his rolling chair, and then noticed his desk drawer was slightly ajar. When he looked inside, he became alarmed when he immediately noticed that his comb was missing from his desk drawer!

With an overly zealous swipe of his arm, he angrily knocked everything off his desk and across his office.

"What sort of Voodoo Gris Gris you up to now, you Cajun rattlesnake!" the Captain harshly exclaimed.

Chapter 11

The compound was inundated by government vehicles, and the crime scene was being heavily investigated.

Each branch of the government was claiming jurisdiction and the local police were also pushing for their own investigation.

The consensus was that it was negligent homicide because the death was caused by a dog.

Captain Landry offered to set up an information conference where they could all sit down and question him over the crime scene.

So far, to most it looked as if it was a dog training exercise that went awry.

The Captain waited as the mess hall filled up with the many branches of crime scene investigators.

When they were all seated the Captain reported:

"Da victim, Lieutenant Parker was a biological and mechanical engineer dat was a member of da US military. He was responsible for creatin' and implementin' military style devices and tools to train canines to behave in a manner dat would benefit da interests of da United States government.

Da Lieutenant was workin' on drugs and mechanisms dat would create aggressive behavior in canines, which would cause dem to ferociously attack on command.

I can't give out all da details, because most of y'all don't have security clearance. But, we are considering a dog mauled da Lieutenant, and it was under control of some sort of experiment gone wrong.

Also, one of my privates is missing.

His name is Private Lester "Tunder" Duponte.

He is a local boy from down in Cajun Arcadiana, my neck of da woods. I don't believe der is a connection wid da Lieutenant's death, and it may just be a coincidence he is missing," stated the Captain.

A police officer stood up and introduced himself as Detective St. Pierre, and directed a statement to the Captain.

"If ya don't mind Captain, we would like to question this Lester Duponte too. Seems kinda odd that he is gone just after a man was killed, so we'll also be lookin' out for him too," stated the officer.

"Dat's up to you, but as I said, no one knows what happened in dat lab," stated the Captain.

The Captain then took a few more questions, and then abruptly left the room.

He was then approached by Private Kozlowski.

"That was pretty vague sir, why didn't you tell them about the "Tiger Shark".

"It was under my care when it got stolen, and I'm gonna get it back. Besides, I'm not 100% sure Duponte had anything to do wid da killing of Lieutenant Parker.

But between me and you, I tink he did, but I'd rather it be us dat go after and find him dan da FBI and da CIA. Dey would shoot him first and ask questions later," stated the Captain.

Private Kozlowski nodded in agreement.

"What are we going to do Captain?" question the Private.

"We are goin' after him! Now get a posse up. We are headin' to da Bayou and I'm gonna get my comb back!" firmly stated the Captain.

Chapter 12

Duponte and Superman had left the military base in the darkness of night, without being seen.

The base was lightly guarded and there were only a few military police stationed at the entrance of the base.

Duponte had cut a strand in the chain link fence in a desolate area in the rear of the base, and the fence easily came apart.

There was a dirt road behind the base which led to a nearby water pumping station, and there waiting was Duffy in his small antiquated pickup truck, idling with the passenger door wide open.

When Duffy noticed Duponte running towards him, he flashed his lights to reveal his whereabouts.

The pair raced over to the vehicle, and Duponte tossed his duffle bag into the truck bed, where there was a live pig rummaging in a cage.

Superman continued on and jumped into the front seat of the truck and layed down leaving no room for Duponte.

"Get in back with the pig, Superman!" Duponte shouted.

Superman planted himself there, and put his head down and refused to ride in back with the pig!

"Hurry up and get in before someone sees us, Tunder!" Duffy exclaimed.

Duponte gave up, and climbed in the back of the truck with the Attache' case in hand, and he sat down next to the caged pig.

The truck then quickly drove off, and Duponte began bouncing all over the truck bed as Duffy raced away down the bumpy dirt road.

Superman occasionally poked his head up, and looked back out the rear window at Duponte, seemingly to rub in the fact that he was sitting up front, while Duponte was stuck sitting in the truck bed with the pig.

It wasn't long before they hit the main road and drove the 50 miles back to Arcadiana.

Duffy finally pulled off the main road and drove down a desolate swamp road to an abandoned stilt house camp where they all exited Duffy's truck.

"Tanks for catchin' on us, Bon ami," rejoiced Duponte.

"No problem, Tunder... So what's going on? You didn't say much when you called and asked me to hijack you off the army base," stated Duffy

Duponte began telling him his story of how Bobo set him up to be killed.

He told him about the Lieutenants gambling debt, and how Bobo used that to strong arm the Lieutenant into killing him. He knew if his own hand was blatantly in on the murder he would pay dearly by way of his mother Lucille, and her strong Voodoo Black Magical powers.

"What are you gonna do now, Tunder?"

Duffy asked.

"Dat's simple, I'm gonna kill Bobo as soon as I find him!" declared Duponte.

"Good luck wid dat, Tunder. Bobo's got his own Voodoo Witch watchin' out for him now. Anything happens to him and you'll get the Gris Gris right back on yourself!" exclaimed Duffy.

Duponte didn't seem very bothered by the situation.

"Who's he got lookin' after him?" questioned Duponte.

"Medusa" replied Duffy.

"Who in Holy Trinity is Medusa?!" inquired Duponte.

"Remember, Gloria Spritzer. Dat skinny girl in middle school dat had a crush on you, Tunder. Dat's Medusa!" he replied.

"Gloria? She's a scrawny kid, I doubt she is strong enough to go against my Mamma. Besides I think she still has da 'Cher Cher' for me," smirked Duponte.

"You ain't seen her in a while, Tunder. People change and der's a reason she calls herself Medusa, you'll see," said Duffy.

Chapter 13

The two men and Superman walked for a short distance down a narrow path, dragging the caged pig towards the water channel.

Hidden under a camouflage tarp was Duffy's gator boat.

They hoisted the pig into the boat, and they all hopped in. Duffy began pulling the starter cord on the boat's motor several times, and it seemed that it was not going to start.

"Mais, you got gas in da tank?" Duponte nervously questioned.

Then on his next pull, the motor instantly revved up.

"Yep, I guess I do!" replied Duffy, and off they went.

They careened through the numerous waterway mazes that criss crossed throughout the Bayou on Duffy's motor boat.

They were heading to Duponte's mother's house.

But, Duponte knew once they had found Lieutenant Parker's body, they would be looking for him, and staying at his mothers was the first place they would look for him and Superman.

Duffy decelerated the boat's motor and they glided to the dock which was located in front of his mother's stilt house.

The yard was eerie, with a slight fog drifting up off the swampy water and it was billowing up around her house.

Pagen Voodoo artifacts were hanging from the trees, and all around her property, and there were skulls and crossbones painted on numerous "Keep Out!" and "No Trespassing!" signs.

Dead petrified chickens, animal skulls and chicken feet tied together with bloody feathers were hanging everywhere, along with the eerie clumps of spanish moss dangling from the swamp trees which made it extremely creepy.

Duponte and Superman quietly exited the boat, and pushed off Duffy back into the waterway.

"Tanks again, Bon ami. I hope to see you at da Boucherie at yo Mamma's!" whispered Duponte.

"You watch out for yourself, Tunder!" replied Duffy.

"Laissez les bon temps roulez!" chuckled Duponte.

The two friends waved goodbye, and Duponte walked up the dock with Superman by his side, lugging his duffle bag and Attache' case.

Chapter 14

Duponte quietly turned the blistered brown ceramic door knob, and slowly opened the old weathered wooden door of his mother's stilt house.

It creaked and squeaked as he tried to quietly enter her pitch dark home.

He carefully tiptoed in with Superman, hoping not to wake her, but was alarmed when he heard the familiar sound of a pump shotgun shell being chambered into its barrel!

"I can kill you with no recourse for breakin' and enterin' into a poor woman's home, and then hang you out to dry on my fence post like a dead raccoon!" an angry woman's voice remarked.

"Don't shoot, Ma! It's me, Lester!"

"What are you doing here, boy?! It's 4:30 in the morning?! I could have cursed y'all into a muskrat, or even worse, shot your butt full of buckshot!" his mother exclaimed.

"I think I'd rather the buckshot than be turned into a muskrat, Ma!" joked Duponte.

"Yeah, I guess I would agree with ya on that one," she chuckled.

"I'm in trouble Ma, I went Awol on account of Bobo putin' a hit on me.

Bobo got his hooks into Lieutenant Parker, and worked him into a big Razzle Dazzle debt. When Bobo found out I was at da Fort wid Lieutenant Parker, he made a deal wid him.

If he killed me, he would wipe his slate clean.

Bobo's still stewin' over dat dog fight he lost.

Da Lieutenant set me up to get mauled by a vicious dawg. He cut the straps on my protective gear and when da Dawg almost had me, he refused to call him off!

Captain Landry ordered da dog killed, just in time.

I couldn't let it go, so I gave Lieutenant Parker a taste of Cajun Justice.

Me and Superman took off, but Landry is a Cajun, and he'll be coming for me, and dis is da first place he will look!" Duponte stated.

"Pay no mind son, you rest here and I'll keep ya safe, but we have to do somethin' about Bobo.

He ain't gonna get away with messin' with my boy," replied Lucille.

"I don't know Ma, Duffy says that he got his own Voodoo Witch watchin' out for him.

Remember Gloria Spritzer from middle school? He says she calls herself Medusa, and she is getting mighty powerful!" declared Duponte.

"Well now, this is gettin' interestin'. I ain't worried about Gloria Medusa. We need to get a hold of something personal dat belongs to Bobo. Like a toothpick or hair brush, so I can make a doll and really 'stick it to him' figuratively speaking," she stated.

"We both know dat's not gonna be easy since he knows what can happen if a Voodoo Witch gets a hold of them.

By da way, here is Captain Landry's comb, I just need to make sure he keeps his hands off of me till I can straighten things out with Bobo," stated Duponte.

His mother took the comb and placed it on a pagan altar that she had set up in her living room.

"Where's Uncle Reggie?" questioned Duponte.

"He's been campin' up at his moonshine hide away all month.

He's up there with Gran Pop. Gran Ma told me they caught a big red wolf that was getting into their food stash, and they got it tied up and have been drinkin' with it all week!

You should go up and see it, and bring Uncle Reggie and Gran Pop some more supplies. It'll be a good place for you to hide out for a while too," she stated.

Duponte nodded his head in agreement.

"Maybe you're right. I can stay dere with dem for a bit. Da Captain will never find me at da camp," he stated.

"Alright, it's late. You get yourself up to bed, but that flea carpet Supermutt has to stay outside," ordered his mother.

Superman, whimpered and dropped his head as he made a sad face, turning on his drooping puppy dog eyes and he sadly whimpered.

"Ohhh okay, you can sleep on da couch. I'm always a sucker for those puppy dog eyes," chuckled Lucille.

Superman dropped his act and his tail began wagging as he eagerly hopped onto the couch and curled up.

"We'll talk more in the mornin', but don't you worry, Lester. I won't let anything happen to ya," she stated, and she kissed him on the cheek and they went to bed.

Chapter 15

Later that morning, Duponte and Superman took their old canoe, and paddled up river to his Uncle's secret moonshine distillery.

It was hidden deep in one of the seldom traveled Bayou swamp channels, and nearly impossible to find.

When Duponte finally arrived at the site, he called out to his Uncle and Grandfather.

"Don't shoot Uncle Reggie, it's me Lester!"

There was suddenly vigorous rustling in the shrubbery in front of him. Then bursting out of the bushes his Uncle appeared!

He blankly staggered out of the brush, clumsily tripping over himself, and he had that "wide eyed, drunken stupor" look about him.

Uncle Reggie was a frail, red faced upper middle aged man with a long scraggly hillbilly beard.

He had lost most of his teeth due to violent fist fights and drunken brawls, mostly during Carnival when he was younger.

It was difficult to understand him without his teeth and his heavy Cajun accent even when he was sober, but it was nearly impossible to understand him when he was drunk.

He wore an open camouflage army flak jacket, which he kept after doing his tour in Viet Nam, revealing several inappropriate shriveled up tattoos on his sweaty chest, and his dirt stained blue jeans were tucked inside his swamp boots.

As he fell out of the brush, he seemed to be inebriated due to his constant "sampling" of his moonshine.

"Hi ya Unkie, Mamma sent me up wid some food for you and Gran Pop, and I was hopin' I can crash wid you for a while?

I went Awol and dey are lookin' for me. I need a place to hide out for a bit," Duponte stated.

His uncle blankly stared at him for a moment, and started drifting forward and backward as if he was going to fall over but kept catching his balance.

"Ho de haw haw busta, wah da who ha, bring it on whoopie, Mao Mao Charlie, blast off! Rue ha!" replied his Uncle.

Duponte just shook his head in confusion, and followed his Uncle as he staggered through the woods blabbering his unrecognisable language all the way back to the encampment.

"Where's Gran Pop?" inquired Duponte as they meandered down a narrow dirt path deeper into the woods.

"He shuken da gulf!" replied Reggie.

When they arrived at the camp, there was a fire burning under an old rusty 50 gallon drum connected to a tall lop-sided conical copper top, and a coil of thin copper tubing attached to the top of it.

It curled around a few times forming several hoops and it ended dribbling clear grain alcohol into an old glass milk bottle.

That was Uncle Reggies moonshine still.

"Where's all the moonshine Uncle Reggie?" Duponte inquired.

Reggie pointed his unstable finger toward Grand Pop who was passed out and his leg was chained to a tree!

There was also a large red wolf tied up next to him, and it too was also unconscious, and laying upside down on Gand Pop's lap!

"Dey drunked it awll! Dat big gulf and him! Dem tic tock up in da rocket ship all drunken apple pie," replied Uncle Reggie.

"You mean dat wolf and Gran Pop done drunk all your moonshine?" Duponte exclaimed.

"Drunk it all as a shoe shine buuzzy bee," burped his Uncle.

Duponte turned to Superman who was now sniffing at one of the empty liquor bottles, and attempting to lap up some of the last drops of the alcohol.

"Hey!! Do you want to end up like dis bunch! Hog tied to a tree and passed out! Never touch dat fire water!" he shouted at Superman.

Superman layed down and put his head on his front leg and covered his eyes with his other leg and made an "Errrrr?" sound as he promised to stay sober.

Chapter 16

Private Kozlowski knocked on the Captain's door.

"Who der!" shouted a testy Captain Landry.

"Private Kozlowski, Sir. I think I might have some useful information about Private Duponte," replied the Private.

"Well don't just stand out dere, get your butt in here!" shouted the Captain.

The Private eagerly entered the Captains office and closed the door.

"What chu got, boy!" the Captain inquired.

"Well Sir, the other day when Private Duponte and I were picking up the mongrel canines from the pound, it was apparent that the Private was friends with the animal control officer. His name was Duffy," stated the Private.

"Ahh yes, Duffy Lemone. Another one of Acadiana's finest degenerates. Is he still rubbin' mayonnaise in his hair?" jeered the Captain.

"Well it was greasy, Sir. But I didn't get close enough to taste his hair," replied the Private.

"Okay, so he knows Duffy, so what?" questioned the Captain.

"Well Sir, I took the liberty to call the pound and Duffy never showed up for work today. I think that maybe this is not a coincidence. He might have been involved in Private Duponte's get away," stated Private Kozlowski.

"You got my attention Private, but do you have anything more substantial than he knew Duffy, and Duffy was too drunk to show up for work today?" sarcastically stated the Captain.

"Well Captain, there is one more thing. While we were at the pound, we noticed a wild hog in one of the cages. Duffy mentioned that there was going to be something called a 'Butchery' at his mother's place this weekend, and he invited us to attend. It might be a good starting place," suggested Private Kozlowski.

"It's called a Boucherie. If he is with Duffy, you are right, it will be a good place to start. But it won't be easy. That is gonna be deep into the heart of Acadiana. Lester's Mamma will be watching out for him, as well as most of the swamp people, on account dey protect der own.

Let me make a few calls to find out where Duffy's Mamma lives," stated the Captain.

"Private Duponte is my friend, Sir. I just don't want to see him get hurt, and I'd like to help to clear his name," stated Kozlowski

"I hear ya Private, lets see what we can do. You did real fine. You are dismissed," stated the Captain.

Chapter 17

The sun was setting over the Bayou, and there were three large pigs roasting on a long wooden spit over an open pit fireplace.

Occasionally Duffy would walk by and baste the hogs, turn the spit and throw another log onto the fire.

There were approximately 85 of the locals there, who were heavily drinking and dancing to Zydeco music, as a small group of friends had brought their instruments and entertained the crowd.

It was a gnarly group, and most of the men, and some women were carrying pistols and large hunting knives, in the event they came across a vicious animal or nesting croc's out in the woods.

Duponte was watching from an old barn that was located on the far corner of the property near the water.

He was patiently watching with Superman by his side, and he had brought the drunkin' red wolf that his uncle had captured at their moonshine camp, which was still hung over and passed out on the barn's wooden plank floor.

Duponte was constantly scanning over the attendants at the party, in hope that Bobo just might show up, considering he knew many of the locals that would be there.

As darkness fell over the Boucherie, Captain Landry and a small group of snipers moved in on the party.

Stealthily watching from the thick underbrush, in their camouflage fatigues and their sophisticated surveillance gear.

With night vision goggles they scanned the area, searching for a sign of Duponte and Superman.

People were coming and going throughout the night by canoe, motor boat, fan boats, pontoon boats and anything else that floated.

The Captain and his men were being eaten alive by mosquitos, and were dodging huge swamp bats that were constantly swooping down at them.

Most all of the soldiers, except for Captain Landry, had no training for being out in the swamp.

They were constantly stepping in mud holes and quick sand, and they were all dreadfully afraid of the poisonous snakes and alligators that were certainly in the area.

"Sir, it's almost midnight and no sign of Duponte. Maybe we should call this one off?" suggested Koslowski.

The Captain held up his finger for silence when he thought he heard the faint sound of a fan boat in the distance that was heading up river, and it was getting louder as it approached.

When it finally arrived near the dock, it's huge engine cut off and it glided to the dock where someone grabbed hold of it's tie off rope and tied it down to a pole.

A large heavy set man wearing a white seersucker suit and boaters hat could be vaguely seen getting off the boat, along with a tall, slender woman who was wearing a long tattered shawl over her shoulders.

They continued on, and walked arm in arm up the wooden dock stairs toward the party.

"Figures you show up right when the food is ready Bobo!" shouted one party goer.

Bobo just smiled and tipped his straw boaters hat, waved his cane and continued toward the food.

Duponte noticed the fan boats arrival, and instantly recognised Bobo by the clothes he was wearing.

One of the snipers suddenly noticed movement coming from the window of the old barn, and confirmed that he had located Private Duponte.

"Okay boys, let's just sit tight and see what dis Lutin (a baby ghost) is up to. Once he makes his move, we'll snatch him!" whispered the Captain.

While Bobo filled his belly with pork and other Cajun fare, his woman was wandering around the perimeter of the party, as if she was looking for someone.

Duffy discreetly passed by Bobo and inconspicuously sprayed a burst of attractant on his seersucker jacket, and quickly returned back to the barn, reported to Duponte and returned the spray bottle to him.

"I did it! I sprayed it where you told me to!" exclaimed Duffy, and he quickly left the barn and returned to the party.

The tall slender woman noticed Duffy leaving the barn, and wandered over to investigate what he had been up to.

Duponte noticed her approach and moved closer to the barn door.

"Hey Gloria!" whispered Duponte.

She was not startled. In fact she was intrigued by the fact that someone was calling her name.

"Who is there? Come on out if you want to play," she maniacally stated.

She reached into her shoulder bag and removed a small jar of magical fireflies and smashed it on the ground!

As it broke the flies were released, and they glowed so brightly that they illuminated the entire area.

Duponte came out from his hiding place and stood in the doorway of the barn, and he came face to face with "Medusa".

"Hi Gloria, long time no see." stated Duponte.

"Well, well, well, if it isn't the infamous, Tunder Duponte in the flesh!" she sarcastically proclaimed.

"Wow! You really blossomed, Gloria. I especially love what you've done wid your hair. Maybe you could have squeezed in a few more dead rattlesnake heads in dat snake nest of yours," Duponte joked.

"I thought I heard you were shoveling up dog poo for the army over at Fort Chips?" she retorted.

"Yes, I was. But not any more, I just didn't like being a chew toy for vicious dogs to play wid. By da way, I couldn't help but notice you linked up with Bobo.

Ain't he kind of old and greasy for you?" questioned Duponte.

"Awe, are you jealous, Tunder? Don't you worry Tunder, he just pays me to watch his back.

You know who my true love is, don't ya, Tunder?" she lewdly implied and winked.

She slowly moved towards him, backing him into the barn when she oddly noticed the red wolf, who was passed out on the floor, and Superman, who was intently watching her from across the room.

"I really love that snake tattoo runnin' up your arm and around your throat, Gloria, it's so realistic," Duponte nervously stated.

She stared seductively into his eyes as she began enchanting him with her black magic.

He was becoming entranced by her vibrating green lizard eyes and succumbing to her cursed spell.

She backed him up against a wall and put her snake like arms around his neck as she caressed his face ever so delicately with her 3" long fingernails.

As she continued moving in on him, she began licking her lips with her hideous forked tongue and she was preparing to kiss him!

By this point he was totally under her spell and in a zombie like state.

Medusa then began grotesquely twisting and stretching her jaw as if to unhinge it as a snake would do prior to consuming large prey.

Then, as she maintained her spell on Duponte, she slowly stretched open her enormous mouth, and suddenly two large glistening fangs dripping with poison revealed themselves as she prepared to drive her poisonous venom deeply into Duponte's neck!

Her forked tongue was slithering about as the venom dripped from her dagger like fangs!

She managed to stretch her mouth open even wider as she prepared to strike her lethal bite!

Then suddenly Medusa heard a "click" sound coming from Duponte's hand, and she had instantly realized that her spell was broken.

"What was that clicking sound?" Medusa sternly asked.

"It's a transmitter. I just activated dat drunkin' red wolf to run off and tear Bobo to pieces for putting dat hit on me. Sorry, I didn't want you getting in da way, Gloria," he replied.

He then revealed an amulet made out of a hollowed out possum head filled with goat hair and an owl claw which was hanging from his neck, hidden underneath his shirt!

It contained the "protection potion" that his mother had concocted for him, and Medusa suddenly realized that he had been pretending, and was not captivated by her black magic at all, and only keeping her attention away from Bobo!

The wolf quickly began to rise and became alert, he sniffed at the air and suddenly charged out of the barn with dire purpose in Bobo's direction.

"If I were you, you should go home now, Gloria. Stop messin' with da Voodoo and clean yourself up. You're a pretty girl underneath all dat crazy junk," Duponte solemnly stated.

"Not on my watch, Tunder! And by the way, my name is Meduusaaaa the Guardian Protector!" she declared.

She lunged at him despiratly trying to grab a few strands of his hair from his head, so that she could obtain a personal item of his, and she could later fabricate a Voodoo doll in his image and torture him to death!

But he was too quick and he pushed her aside.

Her hair flew up, and one of her snake heads fell off from her dreadlocks as she fell to the ground.

Superman became aware of the altercation and quickly got up and began to growl at her.

She threw some sort of witchcraft dust on the ground, which instantly created a green blast of smoke and she was gone!

The red wolf had just zeroed in on Bobo and was racing across the property towards him.

The crowd quickly parted as they noticed the raging wolf heading across the yard towards Bobo, as he was unsuspectedly gorging down a plate of roasted pork and jambalaya!

When Bobo realized that the wolf was coming for him, he panicked and lifted his cane, and prepared to stab the wolf with it.

Desperately he fumbled trying to remove the long sword concealed in his cane as the wolf had just leapt off the ground to attack him!

The wolf latched onto the cane with his powerful jaws and tore it from Bobo's hands.

Then Bobo instinctively grabbed for his snub-nosed revolver but it was too late!

The wolf viciously latched onto his arm and Bobo couldn't aim his pistol!

Bobo was desperately crying for help, but suddenly no one had the sobriety nor the inclination to shoot the wolf!

Actually no one really cared if Bobo did wind up getting mauled to death, considering most of the party goers had been ripped off by him at some point in time.

Suddenly a green cloud of smoke blew up from the ground, and Medusa magically appeared!

She quickly threw a vile of potion at the wolf which exploded and instantly placed him under some sort of demonic spell.

In that instant, the wolf completely froze up and fell to the ground, and he was now in a suspended like state and under Medusa's complete control!

Chapter 18

The Captain was becoming impatient, and decided that they had better move in on Duponte before he escaped.

The Captain and his men began encircling the barn as they were concealed in the thick swamp brush, and were awaiting the Captain's order to ambush Private Duponte in the barn.

The Captain noticed a large wolf quickly exiting the barn and thought that it was odd, and recounted that he had seen "those eyes" before on the canine that was under the influence of the Tiger Shark earlier that week.

The Captain used an electronic megaphone, and ordered Private Duponte to come out of the barn with his hands up, or they would have no choice but to obliterate the barn with bullets.

After a few moments with no response from Private Duponte, the Captain gave the order to his men to begin launching tear gas cartridges into the old barn.

The tear gas shells were bursting throughout the barn's thin walls, as Duponte and Superman ducked down and out through a secret trap door cut into the barn's wooden floor, and followed an escape way down to the dock.

He noticed Bobo's fan boat tied down and the driver was sleeping on the boat's floor as he patiently waited for Bobo's return.

Duponte gave Superman the order to chase Bobo's driver off the boat, and when the man suddenly awoke to the sound of a growling, ferocious dog, he chose to jump into the swamp, and take his chances with the poisonous snakes and alligators rather than Superman!

The pair then jumped onto Bobo's fan boat, and Duponte fired up the engine and the large fan blades began thrusting the boat forward, and they quickly departed the scene.

The Captain and his men continued their assault, until he noticed a fan boat quickly exiting the dock, and saw a dark figure on it waving "Bye Bye" to him.

The Captain, realizing Duponte had just escaped, ordered his men to cease fire, and when they all rushed into the old barn, they discovered the trap door and Duponte's secret escape route to the dock.

The Captain angrily ordered his men to pack up their gear.

"I'll get you another day, Duponte!" shouted the Captain as the mosquito ravaged men hastily gathered their gear, and headed for their boats which were concealed down river.

Chapter 19

Duponte drove the fan boat quickly through the water channels, following the waterways that he grew up traveling on since he was a young boy.

He thought about how powerful Gloria had become, and that she could possibly be stronger than his mother.

He decided he had better return to his mother's house to warn her about Gloria, and to report back on how Uncle Reggie and Gran Pop were doing at the distillery.

As he approached her dock he noticed that her house was dark and something was not right.

There were new animal skulls and chicken bones recently scattered on the dock.

Then he noticed the glint of a light reflecting from someone's rifle scope who was hiding behind her tool shed.

Duponte immediately put the boat in full speed and bolted away from the property.

There was a posse of law enforcement there, waiting for him to show up, led by Detective St.

Pierre, the officer who questioned the Captain at the meeting.

As he sped away, a bright spotlight was directed on him, and a police boat which was concealed in a narrow inlet accelerated after him!

Duponte raced through several water channels with the police boat giving chase and trailing closely behind him with its sirens blaring and police lights flashing.

"Lester Duponte! Stop in the name of the law!!" a loud command blared out from over the police boats PA system.

Then he heard gunshots and bullets flying over his head, and he decided he had enough of this cat and mouse chase. Then out of nowhere he suddenly noticed another police boat charging toward him from the opposite direction with its lights flashing and sirens blaring as well.

He sped onward toward the oncoming Police boat, serpentining over the water, creating a turbulent wake for the police boat chasing behind him, while dodging the bullets being fired at him from both directions!

He was dangerously caught between both police boats, and the police were actually shooting in a crossfire at each other!

A dense eerie fog quickly began to accumulate and it rose up off the water way.

A game of chicken ensued as the oncoming Police boat was heading right towards Duponte!

Duponte would not yield and at the last second the police boat veered out of Duponte's way, avoiding a collision. Suddenly the fog became so dense it was impossible for the police boats to see anything, including Duponte!

They both recklessly swerved right into each other's wake and collided into a massive levee, where both boats were run aground!

Duponted quickly directed his fan boat through the fog, and into a grassy marsh land where the fan boat could easily glide over the swamp, and no one would be able to follow him.

Chapter 20

It was an exceptionally hot and humid morning at the base and Captain Landry was on the phone with the Colonel.

"I promise you Colonel, I will find dat boy, and den I'll have that slippery scoundrel court martialed and hung for goin' Awol!" barked the Captain.

Private Kozlowski entered the Captain's office with a large manila envelope.

The Captain hung up the phone, still quite aggravated after being reprimanded by the Colonel for allowing Duponte to escape from the Boucherie.

"Sir, this just arrived from the reconnaissance department," reported Private Kozlowski.

The Captain quickly opened the envelope, and removed a DVD marked as evidence.

There was a brief letter stating that this was a true copy of the surveillance taken at the Boucherie the past Saturday evening.

The Captain placed the disk into his desktop computer and they both sat down to watch the video.

They watched and fast forwarded through most of the party until they came across Duffy going in and out of the barn several times.

Then the action picked up when they saw Gloria and Bobo arrive on their fan boat.

They watched Bobo as he gorged himself, and Gloria as she wandered around the grounds, and when she walked into the barn, it suddenly illuminated.

A short time later they saw the wolf charging out of the barn, and it headed directly for Bobo when suddenly a burst of smoke appeared and Gloria popped out of it, and she cast a potion upon the wolf which instantly paralyzed it!

"What did I tell you about Voodoo, Private! You see dat Witch...She popped up from nowhere, and stopped dat wolf in his tracks with no gun or tranquilizer! Her powers are stronger dan I ever seen!" stated the Captain.

"Sir, maybe the gentleman in the suit stopped the wolf. He appeared to be trying to stab it with his walking stick," replied Kozlowski.

"No Private, it was Black Magic. We need to pay Duponte's Mamma, Lucille a visit. I don't know why but a strange feelin' is comin' over me, and I'd like to see what she's been up to, and maybe she can help us get her son to surrender himself.

"Sir, are you sure you want to go into the Lion's den?" questioned Kozlowski.

"I haven't seen her in 24 years to be exact, and she hasn't put the Gris Gris on me yet," replied the Captain.

"But your comb, Captain. You seemed to think that she would make a Voodoo doll from your hair which was caught in its teeth? Maybe I should go alone since I am Dupontes friend," stated Kozlowski.

"I'm not worried about that Voodoo doll so much, it couldn't be very powerful with just a few of my hairs.

Go get a Humvee. We are going to da 'Lion's den'," ordered Captain Landry.

Chapter 21

Duffy was passed out on his mother's porch, stretched out on an old stained sofa which has been there as long as anyone could remember.

The morning sun was blaring down on him as he struggled to shield his eyes from its blistering rays and recover from an overwhelming hangover.

Suddenly he felt a hard stick whack him across his stomach, and he was startled as he grabbed his belly in pain and his eyes bulged wide open!

Standing before him, with his gnawed up cane in hand was none other than Bobo, Medusa and one of his ruthless henchmen named Pauly.

Duffy quickly tried to jump up, and he searched for an escape route, but Bobo pushed him back down with the end of his cane, and Pauly had his pistol trained on him.

"Uhh, Hi Bobo, did you have a good time at my Mamma's Boucherie last night?" Duffy nervously asked.

"Why I suuure did. Thank you for youur fine southern hospitality, Duffy. That is, until that mean old wolf came after me," Bobo sarcastically stated.

"Not to be rude, but why are you here, Bobo?" Duffy nervously asked.

"Medusa seems to think that you had somethin' to do with that wolf comin' after me last night. That would be a horrible thought that my friend Duffy Lemone would set me up like that. But I told Medusa that you would never do such a thing like that to a friend, now would ya, Duffy?" sarcastically inquired Bobo.

"I was just as surprised as you were about da wolf and Tunder showin' up at da party. Do you think he had somethin' to do with dat wolf comin' after you?" naively questioned Duffy.

"Duffy, Duffy, Duffy...please don't play that game with me. I know Tunder was at da dawg pound last week...He even stopped off at the Crawdad Shack afterwards. Thanks for sending Milard your Cher. Otherwise, I might not have found out that you two were together that day," stated Bobo.

"Awe Bobo, he just came to da pound to pick up a few mongrels for da base, dat's all! Honest, Bobo!" replied Duffy.

"Duffy, I need you to be a fine citizen and tell me where Tunder and my fan boat are at?!" demanded Bobo.

"I don't know, he's somewhere out in da Bayou," replied Duffy.

"Hmmm, somewhere in the Bayou, huh," remarked Bobo.

Bobo then glanced over at Medusa and nodded to her to take over the interrogation.

She was holding a little rag doll made up of Duffy's greasy black hair, straw and pieces of his clothing.

It resembled Duffy, including the slicked down mayonnaise in it's hair.

Duffy became alarmed when he noticed the resemblance to himself, and he knew exactly what the demonic object was! A Voodoo doll in his image!

Medusa waved the doll in front of Duffy's face, and began chanting a bizarre spell upon it.

Duffy was petrified as she suddenly removed a 6 inch long spike from her hair nest of snakes, and stabbed it into the head of the Voodoo doll.

Duffy immediately clutched his head, and began screaming in excruciating pain until Medusa removed the spike!

"Now that I have your attention Duffy, I'll ask you again, where is Tunder and my fan boat at?!" demanded Bobo.

"I don't know!" cried Duffy.

Once again Medusa clutched the doll and began stabbing the stomach of the doll!

Duffy buckled over and began holding onto his belly as the pain was excruciating!

"Where is he at, Duffy!" shouted Bobo.

"I don't know!" cried Duffy.

Bobo grew impatient and removed a cigar lighter from his jacket pocket, and struck up a flame.

"I'm only gonna ask you once more Duffy. Where is he?" Bobo scowled .

"I swear I don't know, Bobo. If I knew I would tell you!" shouted Duffy in dire excruciating pain.

Bobo proceeded to lite the doll on fire with his lighter, and smoke actually began rising from Duffy's body!

Immediately a burning sensation overcame him, and sweat began pouring from Duffy's skin, and he felt as if he was on fire!

"Stop!! Stop!! Okay, you win! Stop Bobo, please stop! He's up at his Uncle Reggies moonshine camp. Dat's all I know and I don't know where it is!" screamed Duffy.

Bobo removed the flame, and Medusa removed the long needle from the doll's stomach.

"Now was that so hard to say, Duffy? I really don't appreciate being set up by one of my 'friends', Duffy.

But I'll let it go this one time. Now you owe me one," calmly stated Bobo.

"Thanks Bobo, It was a mistake, and it won't happen again!" cried Duffy.

"I'm sure it won't," grinned Bobo.

They left him lying on the sofa as they proceeded down to the water where their motor boat was docked.

As they were entering the boat, Bobo ripped the doll from Medusa's hand, and he purposely threw the Voodoo doll far into the water, where it quickly began to sink down into the slimy swamp water.

Duffy suddenly felt a tightness to his chest and instantly began struggling to breath!

He staggered to his feet clutching at his throat as his face began turning blue!

He gasped, and fought to inhale fresh air as he stumbled off the porch and fell to the ground.

He was desperately clutching his throat and trying to breath! He was drowning, as the doll slowly sank to the bottom of the swamp, and then suddenly he became still.

Duffy was dead.

Chapter 22

The Captain and Private Kozlowski meandered through the narrow water channels which branched out throughout the southern swamp area of the Bayou.

They were getting close to where Lucille's stilt house was situated.

It had been many years since Captain Landry had been back to this portion of the Bayou, and noted how everything had grown in, and the Spanish moss hanging from the trees looked so creepy and spooky.

Finally the two men found Lucille's house and they tied their motor boat to the dock.

"I don't know about this, Captain. This place looks like a scene out of a horror movie! Hand painted 'Keep Out!' signs with skulls and crossbones, dead chicken carcasses and animal skeletons dangling from every tree! Maybe we should go back and get a Catholic Exorcist before we land here!" exclaimed Kozlowski.

"You gotta toughen up boy! What kind of soldier are you? You're afraid of a few dead animal corpses?" reprimanded the Captain.

"Well Sir, after seeing that Voodoo Witch appear from nowhere at the Boucherie, and how she subdued that wolf is making me feel that there just might be something to this Voodoo Black Magic," replied Kozlowski.

Kozlowski then cautiously jumped off the boat, and tied it onto the dock.

They nervously made their way up the rickety wooden steps that went up to the main body of the stilt house.

"Why is this house built on stilts and standing up so high!" stated Kozlowski as he labored up the steps.

"You don't want to be around here where der is a hurricane blowin' through. Da water will rise above its limits and take some of dese houses for a ride!" stated the Captain.

They continued up the stairs onto the porch which surrounded the small rectangular house.

There were all sorts of colorful Hatian artifacts, some antiquated wicker chairs, and all sorts of protective pagen statues and Voodoo artifacts.

The Captain knocked on the old weathered door, and waited while Kozlowski apprehensively scanned the area for ungodly creatures and cursed witches.

Suddenly the door handle began to slowly turn, and the door mysteriously creaked completely open all by itself!

The Captain curiously poked his head in, but there was no one there!

"I'm not so sure about this, Captain!" Kozlowski nervously stated.

"Come on boy! Are you a chicken?!" the Captain taunted.

"No Sir, but by the likes of what I'm seeing here, I don't want to be turned into one either!" the Private nervously proclaimed.

The Captain slowly entered Lucille's lair, as Kozlowski closely followed him from behind, almost climbing on top of the Captain as they walked into the house.

The door quickly slammed shut behind them, and then a violent burst of red smoke began billowing up from the corner of the room.

The two men froze as they watched the smoke dissipate.

Then there, sitting on a massive red velvet throne, wearing a crown made of exotic rooster feathers, golden twine and silver ornaments, with a blue sequin cape draped over her shoulders, royally sat, Lucille.

"You always knew how to make an entrance, Lucille!" exclaimed the Captain.

"Well, well if it isn't my old boyfriend Jean Landry coming back for a second date," sarcastically stated Lucille.

"It's been a long time Lucy. You still look as beautiful as ever," stated the Captain.

Private Kozlowski stood there nervously frozen as the two old friends flirted with each other.

"I want to apologize, I never had a chance to say goodbye to you after dat night at da swamp races. I wasn't sure if you wanted me too, since I drew a blank about dat evening. All I remembered was drinking a soda, and da next ting I knew I was waken' up all mosquito bitten and my mind was blank about da night before," stated Captain Landry.

She slowly stood up and offered her hand to Captain Landry.

He graciously took her hand as if she were the Queen of England, and he ceremoniously kissed her hand despite all the hideous jewelry that was adorned all over her wrist and fingers.

She reached into her cloak as if she had something for the Captain, and returned to him his comb which was taken from his desk.

"I won't be needing this," she calmly stated.

"Well that's a relief, Sir. I thought that maybe she had used that comb to put some sort of Voodoo love spell on you, and that's why you wanted to come out here!" exclaimed Private Kozlowski.

Captain Landry glared at him oddly, then turned his attention back to Lucille.

"I have to make a confession, Jean. I once did put a love Gris Gris on a boy a long time ago….It was at a time when I didn't know any better.

He didn't love me, but I thought I could turn him around with magic. But, my magic at that time was not what it is today, and as the potion wore off by night's end, so did the love affair," Lucille sadly stated.

Captain Landry had an eerie feeling that it was him that she might have been talking about.

"About dat night at da swamp races. I don't remember much, but was I dat boy? I always wondered why I blacked out dat night," the Captain inquired.

"You don't remember because that was a side effect of the potion I slipped into your soda. But you were wide awake, and for that night, we were so much in love with each other," Lucille glowed.

The Captain became embarrassed, and insisted that he didn't remember anything.

"Well, that was a long time ago. I suppose you know why we are here. Where's Lester? If he gives himself up and returns what he took, I can help him. Otherwise it's going to get real bad for him, and he might get himself killed," stated the Captain.

"You wouldn't let anyone hurt your own flesh and blood now, would you, Jean?" questioned Lucille.

The Captain became confused and bewildered, desperately trying to reiterate her words.

"Did you say my own flesh and blood??" the Captain nervously repeated.

"That's right, he's your boy Jean. Didn't you see it in his eyes," she exclaimed.

The Captain collapsed into a chair, and suddenly realized that it was true! Lester was in fact his son!

"Why didn't you ever tell me! I had a right to know!" the Captain shouted.

"I didn't want you to think that just because we had a child together that I wanted something from you. There were times that I wanted to write to you, and tell you the truth. But I was afraid you would charge in and take him away from me, on account of my Voodoo religion and all," she stated.

The Captain was angry that he had been the target of her witchcraft which resulted in them having a child, but quickly realized fighting about it now wouldn't change a thing.

"Now that you know he is your son, how are you going to help him get out of this mess?" inquired Lucille.

"It's a big problem. He took revenge on an innocent officer and killed him. He stole a top secret device and used it to committee da murder, and stole Superman which is da property of da United States government. And he took my comb!!" exclaimed the Captain.

"Sir, I think there is more to the story about the Lieutenant. It was apparent that the Lieutenant refused to call off the dog when the animal was clearly seconds away from killing Private Duponte, Sir," stated the Private.

"That's right Jean, there is more to this story. That Lieutenant of yours had accrued a large gambling debt with that crook Beauregard Bobbit, in a Razzle Dazzle game he got suckered into.

Bobo had also lost a large sum of money. Over $60,000 on a dog fight in which Tunder's dog, who was severely beaten, got a second wind, and turned around and beat Bobo's dog right at the bell.

Bobo was angry and thought his dog should have won, but they gave it to Tunder. When Bobo found out that Tunder was assigned to Fort Chips, he came up with a scheme for the Lieutenant to kill him, and in return he would wipe his debt clean!" exclaimed Lucille.

Kozlowski instantly recalled the conversation he had with Duponte in the infirmary, where Duponte told him about the Tiger Shark device the Lieutenant had invented.

"Sir, that makes sense why the Lieutenant requested Duponte in the field for the trial, and then he refused to call off the dog," stated Kozlowski.

The Captain listened intently and the picture was beginning to come clear.

"So, do you tink Tunder went after da Lieutenant for revenge?" questioned the Captain.

"Actually Captain, it wasn't Private Duponte that killed the Lieutenant, it was a dog. In fact sir, the canine didn't even belong to him, and it would be difficult to prove that the dog was actually under the influence of the Tiger Shark without the animal in hand. It could have just been an experiment gone awry by the Lieutenant. All the Private has notably done so far was taken a combat canine for water training without permission. The Tiger Shark Attache' could have just been "misplaced" if we get it back, Sir," Kozlowski craftily stated.

The Captain pondered a moment and turned to Lucille.

"I'll try my best to get dis "misunderstanding" all straightened out, but we need to do it right away. Where is he Lucy?" questioned the Captain.

"He's up at da moonshine camp with my brother Reggie and my Poppa. I'm worried that Bobo and his young Voodoo Witch, Medusa will try to kill him since he no longer has any fear of me," declared Lucille.

"Let's go talk to him. Does he know dat I'm his father?" inquired the Captain.

"No, he believes that his Poppa was killed by a gator when he was just a baby. It will be a surprise to him too!" replied Lucille.

The Captain nodded his head, and the three of them quickly left the house and headed for the dock.

"Don't you worry Lucille, I'm gonna make dis right," stated the Captain.

Then they all entered the boat, and Kozlowski started the motor and off they went, as Lucille guided the way through the maze of channels to the moonshine camp.

Chapter 23

Private Duponte was still asleep at his Uncle's moonshine camp, and lucidly dreaming inside his mosquito tent when he felt the presence of a warm body laying next to him.

He reached over and ran his fingers though soft hair and as he snuggled in closer he whispered sweetly in French;

"Tes cheveux sont si doux, embrasse-moi bébé," (Your hair is so soft, kiss me baby).

He continued caressing the hair of his love as he began to pucker up his lips, when he suddenly felt a big wet drooling tongue licking his face, and he was slobberly awakened from his dream!

Superman was lying there next to him, and finally decided enough was enough, and had to wake him up, before Duponte started kissing him on the snout!

"Uhhhgg! Blah! Disgusting!" Duponte shouted as he jumped up and wiped the dog spit off his face with his shirt sleeve!

Superman seemed to snicker as he watched Duponte struggle to wipe his face clean.

"Really Superman?!!" Duponte shouted.

Uncle Reggie heard the commotion and came staggering out of the woods holding a bottle of moonshine and a roll of toilet paper.

"What de stinger, blister, boom boom away?!" slurred Reggie.

Superman and Duponte both watched as he staggered and stumbled into the camp, and then he suddenly tripped over his own feet and fell to the ground!

The bottle of moonshine shattered against the rocks surrounding the fire pit, and the alcohol caused a giant flare up!!

Out of the blazing fire rose a square piece of parchment paper wavering up with the smoke from the inferno.

Duponte quickly retrieved the smoldering piece of paper, and immediately put out the flames that were consuming it.

It was a message from Bobo!

It stated that they should have a pow-wow meeting that night to peacefully clear up this matter like gentlemen, and put all of this misunderstanding behind them.

He stated that he would be alone, and waiting on the dock next to his shrimp trawler boat "The Drunken Zombie", which was docked on the inlet canal near the old water pump house #64, and Duponte should come alone as well.

"Uncle Reggie, who gave you dis message in da bottle?" inquired Duponte.

Reggie just pointed up to the sky and mumbled,

"Hup der, kabooey" and he hit himself on top of his head.

"Bobo wants a meeting wid me tonight, but I know it's going to be a trap and he'll try to kill me. But dis will never end until one of us goes down, and it ain't gonna be me!" stated Duponte.

Superman became anxious, and began tugging at Duponte's shirt implying he shouldn't go.

"Don't worry my friend, I'm taking you wid me!" stated Duponte.

Chapter 24

Medusa was busily conjuring up potions and spells in her sadistic kitchen of evil, as Bobo and his henchman prepared for the showdown with Duponte at their base camp.

"Bobo, do you really think Tunder is going to show up at the boat dock tonight?" asked Pauly.

Bobo took off his straw boaters cap, and wiped the sweat from his brow with a crumpled up yellow stained white cotton handkerchief.

"He'll come alright. He ain't gonna rest until he gets even with me for putting the hit on him.

But I'll be ready. Medusa has a surprise in store for that Cajun boy, and it will put an end to him and his crazy Voodoo Mamma," replied Bobo.

Medusa could be heard chanting a spell and placing strange herbs, potions and odd animal parts into a large iron cauldron which was dangling by 3 blackened chains over a blazing fire.

Steam was billowing up from the bubbling brew as Medusa meticulously stirred and continued on with her sinister chanting.

"So what's the plan boss? Are we just going to shoot him in the back when he gets there like we usually do, or are we going to drop a trawling net on him, and torture him for a while before we kill him?" maniacally questioned Pauly.

"Settle down Pauly. Those are really good ideas, but those sort of things that we usually do, won't work on Tunder. He has protection from his mamma.

I'll bet he won't show up without her, and it's going to be a showdown between the two witches.

Medusa has ten times the power of Lucille now, and we'll finally be rid of both of them for good. Then I'll take over the entire Bayou!" exclaimed Bobo.

The men gathered some supplies and drove off to the "The Drunken Zombie" to prepare for the meeting.

When they finally arrived at the dock, the two men hopped onto the deck of the large boat, and Pauly opened an ice chest filled with drinks and helped himself to an ice cold can of beer.

He popped it open, and began drinking it as he headed for the door to the storage compartment below.

But when he pulled on the door latch, a loud vicious growl projected out from behind the door, and a massive vicious wolf head snapped at him as he quickly shoved the door closed!

It startled Pauly to the extent that he spilled his beer all over himself!

"What have you got down there, Bobo?! A rabid monster!?" exclaimed Pauly.

"What happened to your pants? Did you wet yourself, Pauly?! Why don't you go down there and make friends," chuckled Bobo.

Pauly jerked back and made it clear that he was not going to do that, and he hastily threw his empty beer can recklessly onto the dock.

"That there is my insurance policy. If everything goes right tonight you will be witness to something extraordinarily extraordinary," stated Bobo.

Pauly was confused and just shrugged his shoulders, and placed the supplies in the ship's cabin.

Then the two men left the boat and drove back to their base camp.

Chapter 25

The small motor boat carrying Captain Landry, Lucille and Private Koslowski carefully meandered through the water channels and side inlets of the Bayou.

Until Lucille finally directed them into the hidden inlet that led to her brother's moonshine camp.

They passed several hand painted signs warning people to go away.

One sign read;

"NO TRESPASSING...SURVIVORS WILL BE SHOT AGAIN!!".

And, as they continued further along, there was another sign that read;

"IS THERE LIFE AFTER DEATH?...TRESPASS HERE AND YOU'LL FIND OUT!!!".

Kozlowski was becoming extremely nervous, and afraid that they may be shot at for trespassing.

"Sir, I'm concerned that we could be shot and killed, considering we are sitting ducks in this small open boat!" exclaimed Kozlowski.

"Don't you worry about that soldier, when Reggie is makin' his moonshine, he's too drunk to shoot straight!" chuckled Lucille.

Lucille then directed the Captain to drive the boat into a dense wall of brush which instantly swung back, revealing a cove with a dilapidated landing dock.

Bobo's fan boat, which Duponte had stolen the night of the Boucherie, was docked there and the Captain headed toward it.

Kozlowski quickly jumped onto the dock and tied off the boat as the Captain helped Lucille out.

Lucille cupped her hands around her mouth and sounded off a vocal signal to the men at the camp, and began calling out the sound of an Egret.

"Whoooop, whoop….Whoop, whoop," she shouted.

About a minute later, they heard the bushes begin to shake and rustle, and then Reggie came stumbling out of the brush.

He was stunned when he realized his sister was there with the Captain and Private Kozlowski.

"What da blubber kooz koo cockle doo!" exclaimed Reggie.

"It's alright Reggie. The Captain is here to help his "son" get out of this mess. Where is Tunder?" questioned Lucille.

"I'm right here," dismally stated Duponte as he was following behind his Uncle through the brush.

It was an awkward moment as Duponte overheard his mother state that the Captain was indeed his father.

"Lester dis is as shocking to me as it is to you! I just want to say dat I never knew dat you were my son, and I was never told about you!" stated the Captain as he gave Lucille a hard stern look of disapproval.

"Mamma, is dis some kinda joke! Der is no way he could be my Daddy, He's so ugly and I'm so handsome!" exclaimed Duponte.

"I promise you, even though you might not see much resemblance and you inherited my good looks and not his, he is your Daddy!" exclaimed Lucille.

The Captain became insulted as they were speaking about him as if he wasn't there.

"Hello? I'm standing right here, and I think I am rather handsome! Don't you agree, Kozlowski?!" the Captain barked.

Kozlowski shrugged his shoulders and awkwardly nodded his head in agreement.

"Okay settle down Jean, you are handsome too," sarcastically patronized Lucille.

"I just want to help you get out of dis mess, Son. I heard dat Bobo put a hit out on you, and dat da

Lieutenant was under his thumb. If you come in, I tink I can explain to da Colonel dat it was just a misunderstanding, and as long as we get da Tiger Shark back. I believe everything will be alright, and we can try to put da pieces back together, and start livin' like a real family," pleaded the Captain.

Duponte glanced at his Uncle Reggie as he took another long swig from his near empty bottle of moonshine.

"What should I do Uncle Reggie?" questioned Duponte.

"Hup, two, rockin brew, kazoo!" stated Reggie.

Duponte nodded his head in agreement and whistled for Superman.

He slowly came stumbling and staggering through the shrubbery, lugging along the metal Attache' case by the handle in his mouth, and he dropped it in front of the Captain.

The Captain leaned down, and patted Superman on the head as he took hold of the Attache' case and then became concerned.

"I tink I smell liquor on dis canine's breath," stated the Captain.

Duponte gave Uncle Reggie a seething stare when he realized he had been pouring moonshine into Superman's water bowl.

Reggie took a bow of remorse, and backed off into the shrubbery and disappeared.

The Captain handed the metal Attache' case to Private Koslowski, and ordered him to take the boat and return with it to his office, where he could change his story that it wasn't stolen, and that he actually misplaced the Attache' case and it was never really missing.

"I'm glad to see that you are alright Duponte. Maybe when dis is all over we can finish that bucket of crawdads we started at the Crawdad Shack," said Private Kozlowski.

"You can bet on it, Koz. Tanks for coming here and saving me from dis bunch of alcoholics!" chuckled Duponte as he glared down at Superman.

Private Kozlowski quickly left with the Attache' case and took a scribbled map with directions from Lucille of how to get back through the channels, and return back into the main waterway.

Chapter 26

"Mamma I have somethin' to tell you. I got a message dat magically appeared out of one of Reggies moonshine bottles. It was from Bobo. He wants me to meet him tonight at da docks where he keeps his shrimp trawler boat.

I know it's a trap, but I need to finish tings wid him, and I know it's not gonna be easy. He has Medusa-Gloria watchin' out for him, and after what I saw at da Boucherie, her magic is very strong...maybe stronger dan yours, Ma," stated Duponte.

"I'll call in da Po-Po to arrest Bobo for puttin' da hit on you, Son. Der is no need to go to a rigged meetin' wid Bobo where we all know it's gonna be a trap!" exclaimed the Captain.

Duponte glanced over at his mother who completely understood the situation.

"It's more than just settling a problem between the two men. It is a fight for power over the Bayou. If Bobo wins, their evil intentions will plague the Bayou forever. If Tunder wins, there will be peace and tranquility for all that live here. Besides, Bobo has the Po-Po in his back pocket, so we are all on our own.

We have to be ready for them, and expect a lot of Voodoo Black Magic!" exclaimed Lucille.

The Captain nodded his head, and understood that this showdown had come to a head, and it had to happen tonight.

"What can I do?" questioned the Captain.

"I'll need you to watch my back tonight...Dad," Duponte smiled.

The Captain put his arms around his son and hugged him.

"I'll be der. Nobody, especially dat Medusa witch is gonna hurt my boy," stated the Captain.

They immediately left on the fan boat, and they returned back to Lucille's home.

"I've got some work to do before tonight," stated Lucille.

"Mamma, I might have someting dat might help!" exclaimed Duponte.

He reached into his shirt pocket and removed the rattlesnake head that he had found that had fallen out of Medusa's hair, when she attacked him in Duffy's barn.

"This belongs to Gloria, Mom," stated Duponte.

She took the dried snakehead and grinned.

"Oh yes, this will do quite well. I have just the recipe to make something nice for Gloria, out of this possession of hers," Lucille chuckled.

"Common Dad, I want to show you something," stated Duponte.

The Captain followed his son to his room where it was filled with all sorts of sport trophies and high school achievement awards.

"I just want you to see dat I am not a total loser, and dat I did real good, just Ma and me. But I had to make money, and da only way I knew how was da swamp way," stated Duponte.

"I'm really proud of you, son and from now on, I'll be der for you," stated the Captain.

"I want to show you somethin' else," stated Duponte.

He lifted a few loose floorboards, and revealed a pair of high tech compound bows with a number of razor bladed hunting arrows and several armament arrows with explosive heads attached to the shafts.

"We are gonna need some heavy artillery for tonight," stated Duponte.

The Captain picked up one of the bows and proficiently drew it back as he aimed it at an imaginary foe.

"It's been a while since I used one of dese. When I was a teenager we used to bow hunt gators out of season when we didn't want da Game Warden to catch us huntin'. Where did you get dese armorment arrows?" questioned the Captain.

"While I was at bootcamp, I became friends wid a soldier responsible for munitions at da base. He sold me all sorts of explosives," replied Duponte.

Lucille called to the men, and they returned to the living room.

Lucille was holding a soft red gingham sack filled with all sorts of black magical potions and mysterious Voodoo objects.

"We are gonna finish them once and for all tonight.

I have a surprise in store for that crew, and Superman is gonna be the Super star!" confidently stated Lucille.

Superman lifted his head when he heard his name, but then retired back to his comfortable nap on the couch.

"I'll fill up da boat wid gas and we'll head over to da docks after sundown," stated Duponte.

"Sounds like a plan," replied the Captain.

A few hours later, the fan boat was idling and ready to go.

Duponte placed their weapons inside the boat, as Lucille finalized her potions.

The sun began to set, and they were on their way, off to the boat dock where they were meeting up for the bitter showdown with Bobo.

As they careened through the narrow inlets and passages of the Bayou, they were all mostly silent except for Superman, who couldn't help barking every time an alligator snapped its tail as it darted away from their boat.

Large ominous thunder clouds began to roll in, and winds began to pick up as they could see the illuminated dock in the distance.

Duponte drove the boat into a small inlet clearing where the Captain and Lucille could get off without being seen and then he continued on to the dock.

They made their way over to a tall antiquated water tower, which was approximately 200 feet from the dock.

The Captain and Lucille then climbed up on a thin wrought iron ladder approximately 100 feet to a narrow platform which surrounded the large water tank.

The Captain positioned himself on the platform with a bow and several explosive arrows, as Lucille began chanting a Voodoo spell and placed herself into a zombie-like trance. Her eyes suddenly began to glow as her pupils rolled back into her skull!

She then ceremoniously extended her arms above her, and with her two hands she began spinning her fingers around her head imitating a cyclone!

Lightning bolts could be seen in the distance along with the muffled sound of thunder trailing a few seconds thereafter. Duponte slowed the fan boats motor as he careened around Bobo's trawler and headed closer toward the dock. As he approached the dock, it seemed to be desolate.

He cautiously maneuvered the boat parallel to the dock, and threw a looped tie down rope over a short pole.

Duponte and Superman quickly jumped out of the boat with his bow and arrows in hand, and quickly scurried across the dock, and they hid behind a stack of drying shrimp nets.

Superman immediately began sensing danger, and became postured for warfare, and positioned himself boldly at Duponte's side as they steathfully made their way closer to Bobo's boat!

They ducked behind poles and shrimp barrels, cat and mousing their way until they were positioned right behind a stack of old wooden cargo crates, which were located a few meters away from "The Drunkin' Zombie".

Chapter 27

Earlier that evening, Bobo had instructed Pauly to climb up the rope ladder that led up to the boom outrigging on top of the boat's shrimp net transom, and to hide in the elevated shrimp nets with a high powered rifle.

"If anything goes Tunder's way….kill him right away!" ordered Bobo.

"What about all this 'hoop la' with Medusa? I thought she was supposed to take out Tunder?" questioned Pauly.

"She is in charge of killing Lucille, and when she is done with her, she is supposed to kill Tunder too. But she has affection for him, and she might just change her mind, and put some sort of Voodoo hex on me instead. Once Lucille is dead, if she doesn't finish off Tunder, shoot him right away, then shoot Medusa. You got that Pauly!?" exclaimed Bobo.

Pauly nodded his head and climbed up the tall rope ladder with his rifle slung over his shoulder up to the boom outrigging, and he hid in the elevated shrimp net, positioning himself for a clear shot down at the dock.

They waited patiently as the sun set and darkness fell over the Bayou.

A full moon shed light on the dock, and hazy steam began to rise off the quiet water.

"Don't you fall asleep up there, Pauly!" scolded Bobo.

Pauly made a facetious snoring sound and chuckled.

"I don't think they are going to show up. He's got to know it's a trap. This is a big waste of time," complained Pauly.

"Just mind your business, and do what I told you!" replied Bobo.

Pauly let out a sarcastic grunt, and chambered a bullet into his rifle as Bobo stood and watched from the bridge cabin of his boat, waiting for Duponte to show up.

Chapter 28

About an hour had passed since sundown, when Bobo decided to leave the safety of the boat's bridge cabin.

He positioned himself in open view on the dock beside his boat to show himself, and that he was seemingly all alone. Suddenly he heard a loud spinning noise coming from up top the old water tower.

He looked up and noticed a dense red and blue smoke cloud forming, and it began swirling around an object up on the service deck of the tower.

The whirlwind began to lift off the tower's platform and then like a micro tornado, traveled down through the air towards the dock.

When it finally landed, it was but a few yards away from him!

The magical smoke slowly cleared, and Bobo was stunned to see Lucille standing there, with her hands still swirling around her head, chanting some sort of powerful Voodoo spell.

She was dressed in a flowing black shredded dress with a yellow scarf wrapped like a turban around her head and she was resembling a yellow hornet.

Her red gingham sack was over her shoulder, and she held a handful of strange rocks and small amulets.

Duponte and Superman boldly came out from behind the crates, and positioned themselves behind his mother!

He had a single arrow locked into his bow, and he aimed it at Bobo.

His mother continued chanting as Bobo nervously stood there.

Suddenly, a blast of green dense smoke began swirling from the open doorway of the shrimp boats storage cabin! When the smoke cleared, Medusa the "Guardian Protectress" was sadistically positioned there!

She held her hands up as if she were a clawing lioness, and her mouth was hideously opened wide, as her grotesque forked tongue wavered about tasting the air for Lucille's scent!

Giant venomous fangs protruded out of her unhinged mouth, as her toxic poison slathered out of them!

Her colorful snake headed dread locks had come to life, and her head was now covered with dozens of live venomous snakes that were protruding from her skull, and they were all hideously slithering and striking out in all directions!

The red wolf suddenly appeared next to her, patiently poised by her side as if in some sort of trance, waiting patiently for its masters command!

Both witches began loudly chanting Voodoo spells, and throwing exploding handfuls of black magical dust into the air!

Lucille positioned herself so as "not to look" at Medusa's hideous head of snakes, fearing that it's ugliness, as legend had it, could in fact turn her or anyone who looks at it into stone!

"Don't look at her head!!" Lucille shouted out.

Electrical sparks and fire then began swirling around Superman.

He began to swell and increase in size, as muscles began protruding from his growing body!

A black cloud of smoke began forming around the red wolf as a whirlwind began to rise up, and then it engulfed the animal!

It spun faster and faster as Medusa used her powerful witchery to begin transformation of the wolf!

"Gloria is too strong! Let's get out of here!" Duponte shouted to his mother over the loud wind.

But Lucille only concentrated deeper, and used all her strength to conjure up even more power!

Duponte glanced over at Superman and noticed through the fire that he was still growing and transforming into a massive muscular Bear-Dog beast, with massive bone crushing teeth and huge bear like claws protruding from his giant paws!

The red wolf was also quickly changing and it began to rise up on its rear two feet, and his body began to stretch and grow, forming long hairy human arms, hands and fingers with razor sharp claws and muscular wolf-like legs!

Its head stretched and contorted into a monsterous half human, half wolf head, with a mouth full of blood curdling razor sharp teeth!

Both Superman and the wolf were shape shifting, and transforming into completely different creatures!

They were no longer a simple dog and a wolf, but now the red wolf was transforming into a savage Rou Gareau!!

Hideously standing upright on two legs, drenched with vicious ferocity and thirsting to kill!

And Superman was transformed into a massive Grizzly Dog with powerful muscles and giant bone crushing teeth!

The two creatures squared off at each other, as Duponte raised his bow at the viciously crazed Rou Gareau!

He aimed his arrow right for the animal's heart, but when he released the arrow, Medusa, with a twitch of her eye brow, directed it away, and it struck a post right next to Bobo's head!

Bobo quickly scurried back onto his shrimp boat, and ran towards the bridge cabin!

Duponte noticed him running away and quickly leapt onto the boat and chased after him!

He dove through the air and tackled Bobo, turned him over and then hit him hard with his clenched fist, squarely on the side of his face.

Duponte jumped on top of him, and began punching him incessantly, but his hands suddenly became too heavy and he couldn't move them.

Medusa had glanced over at the two men who were fighting, and she once again aimed her eyebrow at Duponte projecting a sinister restraining force on him as she continued concentrating her powers on the wolf.

Bobo seized the opportunity and then began beating Duponte with his cane.

Captain Landry up in the water tower, was frustrated at not being able to release a clean shot.

He aimed his bow at the men, but only had the exploding arrows, and feared that by shooting at Bobo, he could blow up everyone on the dock!

And so he painfully watched on, as Bobo continued beating his son!

The two animals were squaring off, and then suddenly they violently attacked each other in a ferocious brawl!

The Rou Gareau was much taller than Superman, and was lashing out with his gigantic claws and large snapping teeth as Superman courageously fought the beast back with his powerful arms and massive bite!

The Rou Gareau became even stronger and substantially larger as Medusa strengthened her spell on it.

The beast then gave out an ungodly howl and began driving Superman toward the edge of the dock!

Then he jumped up in the air and pile drove down on top of Superman's head, knocking him unconscious!

The Rou Garou claiming victory, climbed on top of Superman's lifeless body, pinning him down as he prepared to thrust his clawed fist mercilessly into Superman's chest, to tear out and devour his beating heart!

He then raised his claw upwards toward the full moon, reaching high over his head!

Then he projected a devilish howl as he prepared to drive his claw downward into Superman's chest!

Captain Landry launched one of his exploding arrows at the beast, and it exploded against his body, but it did little damage and only infuriated the beast even more!

The blast though was just enough to barely awaken Superman.

He shook off his daze, and realized the compromised position he was in!

He twisted out from under the beast and lunged for its muscular neck and he grabbed hold, and sunk his massive teeth into the Rou Gareau's hairy throat and then flipped the beast over him!

The Rou Gareau howled in excruciating pain as Superman dug his teeth deeper into its neck!

With his last ounce of strength Superman threw himself off the dock and into the water, dragging the beast off with him!

As they both crashed into the water, it made an unusually large splash, but Superman held his bite tightly as he dragged the hideous beast downward into the depths of the black water, and they both disappeared into the darkness of the Bayou.

The water instantly began to boil, and violently churn, and then everything became quiet, and it appeared that both of them were gone.

Bobo was mortified, as once again Tunder's beast who was down and out, had revived itself to come back and defeat his monster for a second time!!

And Superman had sacrificed his life for Duponte.

Lucille then reached into her sack, and removed a small Voodoo doll resembling Medusa.

Its colorful dreadlocked hair contained the wicked snake head that Duponte had taken from her in Duffy's barn.

Medusa was instantly taken aback when she noticed the little doll that resembled her, and she realized what it was!

Suddenly the storm she was creating immediately dissipated.

Lucille then removed a tiny strand of magical thread from her head wrap, and bound the dolls tiny little arms together! Medusa uttered a wicked shriek, as her arms became instantly paralized, and her eyes were enraged with anger. Lucille began a magical chant and focused all her energy on the doll.

The massive snake tattoo that stretched across Medusa's body, suddenly began to vibrate and miraculously rise off her skin!

The tattoo had come to life, and the giant snake began coiling itself around Medusa's body, constricting her so that she couldn't move until she was totally engulfed by the snake and she became powerless!

The snake then opened its massive mouth and devoured all the smaller snakes protruding from her head, and then it continued on consuming all her Voodoo incantations!

Lucille continued chanting over the doll, and the massive snake continued constricting her, squeezing all the evil and wicked Voodoo from her body.

Now, she was totally stripped clean of all her Voodoo powers, possessions and body disfigurements, and then all that was left of her powers was nothing!

Gloria instantly became unconscious and went limp.

The snake released its grip on her, and she slipped through its coils and fell onto the deck of the boat.

The giant snake then quickly slithered away over the rail of the boat, and disappeared into the murky water.

Duponte's hands suddenly came alive and he grabbed Bobo's cane and pulled it away from him, and the tides turned and then he began beating Bobo with it!

"Hurry up!! Shoot him!! Then kill the Witches!" Bobo desperately shouted up to Pauly.

As Duponte glanced up, he saw Pauly up in the boom net aiming his rifle at him.

Lucille raced over to shield him but she was too late!

The bullet was faster than Lucille and her magic.

Pauly had shot Duponte and he recklessly fell off the boat and into the water! Pauly then quickly took aim at Lucille.

Gloria slowly started to awaken, when she heard Bobo's order to "Kill the Witches" and she realized that Bobo had double crossed her.

She looked up into the dangling shrimp nets, and she saw Pauly taking aim at Lucille with his rifle!

"Lucille! Look out!" Gloria shouted.

Pauly pulled the trigger for a second time, but Lucille had magically vanished off the dock before the bullet could hit her!

Bobo ran off to the bridge cabin and started the boat's diesel engine, as Pauly now turned his attention to Gloria.

As the boat began quickly pulling away from the dock, Pauly aimed his rifle at Gloria who was now desperately running along the dockside searching for Duponte in the murky black water.

As Pauly took aim at Gloria, he slowly began squeezing the rifle's trigger, when suddenly Pauly began having a violent convulsion and couldn't aim his rifle, or pull the trigger!

Lucille had suddenly reappeared on the dock, shaking an empty beer can that she picked up. It was Pauly's can, and she was vigorously shaking it!

He quickly fell from the boom transom, landing hard on the ship's deck, and continued on having a violent convulsion!

The boat's engines shifted into high gear and the boat began swiftly leaving the dock!

Captain Landry stood poised upon the water towers platform, and calmly drew back his compound bow and consecutively released 3 exploding arrows, one after another, into the shrimp boats bridge cabin!

The arrows hit their mark and exploded on impact, and completely obliterated the entire shrimp boat into a massive fiery explosion!

Large pieces of the ship's cabin were falling down from the sky all around them, splashing down into the open waters of the Bayou. And then... there was silence.

Chapter 29

There was a tumult on the water's surface near the dock! The spell had worn off, and Superman surged up from the water's depts and was struggling to pull Duponte up to the dock.

Gloria and Lucille quickly ran over, and pulled him out of the water, and Duponte collapsed into Gloria's arms, while Lucille began chanting a Voodoo healing spell over her son. Captain Landry rushed over and quickly lifted Superman out of the treacherous water, just as an overzealous alligator was on its way and nearly upon Duponte!

He examined Superman for any injuries, but besides a few bumps and scrapes, he seemed fine.

Slowly Duponte began opening his eyes and when he realized it was Gloria holding him, he uttered;

"Ya know Gloria, You're a pretty girl wid out all dat Voodoo junk all over you."

Gloria smiled and brought Duponte closer and hugged him tightly.

"Ya know what, Tunder. I don't need no magic to make you mine," and she leaned over and kissed him.

He smiled back at her and slowly closed his eyes.

The Captain, followed by Superman rushed over to Lucille as she was kneeling next to her son and Gloria.

She quickly stood up as Captain Landry approached and they embraced.

"I want to tell you somethin Lucy. I never told you dis, but I was in love wid you too. But I was just a kid, and I was scared of you! You were so confident and aggressive, I didn't know what to do, so I ran away and joined da Army. I figured I would come back someday when I was a man, and make you my woman," stated the Captain.

"I suppose today is the fine day," joyfully replied Lucille.

And she tightly grasped a tiny pair of dolls that were hidden in her sack.

One of which had the Captain's real hair that she had removed from his comb, and the other doll which was made with her own hair.

They were wrapped together in a red satin bow with other small tokens of love.

As the fog began to lift, Superman noticed the red wolf rigorously swimming across the narrow channel. He climbed out of the water onto shore, where he vigorously shook himself off, and immediately ran into the woods and disappeared.

The Bayou was now at peace….

Chapter 30

The Date: November 4, 2006
The time: 0600 hours (6 AM).

Steam was gently rising off the dew drenched training field as the activities were once again underway at Fort Chips.

Things seemingly returned back to normal at the Fort, and Private Duponte was cleared of all wrongdoing when the evidence was presented before a military tribunal.

No one could find the missing animal linked to the killing of Lieutenant Parker.

Sadly though, Private Kozlowski, along with the Attache' case containing the Tiger Shark, never made it back to the base after leaving Uncle Reggie's moonshine camp.

A massive military search party ensued, including the Coast guard, but the Bayou was so great and vast that it was nearly impossible to find him.

There was lots of speculation, and some suspected he was unable to follow Lucille's scribbled directions out of the maze of channels, and then he either ran out of gas or collided with something that might have sunk his boat.

Possibly he went on land and was tragically attacked and eaten by a large alligator or bitten by a poisonous snake.

Some also suspected that he might have been robbed, shot and murdered if he accidentally came across another Cajuns illicit hideout camp.

Unfortunately for Private Kozlowski, it seemed that it would become an unsolved mystery and no one may ever know what had happened, or find his body.

Chapter 31

 "Sir! Private 1st Class Lester Duponte and Sergeant Major Superman reporting for lunch, Sir!" sarcastically stated the Private as he entered the Captains office.

He comically stood at attention and bestowed a crisp salute to the Captain who was putting a file away in a nearby file cabinet.

Superman was by his side and also stood at attention and seemingly attempted to salute him as well by lifting his paw on to his forehead.

"At ease, you two jokers. And just one more ting Lester and Superman. Don't let dose promotions go to your thick skulls! I had to make a lot of phone calls, and do a lot of butt kissin' to get you dose promotions and straighten out dat whole mess of jambalaya you two put me through," stated the Captain.

"Speaking of jambalaya, Sir. I tink you should take your boy out to lunch!" joked Duponte.

Duponte then ordered Superman to sit on the floor, but instead he hopped up onto the Captain's chair and placed his front paws onto the Captain's desk.

"Oh, so "you" want to be in charge, Sergeant Major Superman?" inquired the Captain.

Superman looked down at the filthy floor and barked a few short barks to the Captain.

"Hey Tunder, Superman wants you to go get a bucket and mop and wash da crap off my floor," stated the Captain.

Duponte was instantly taken aback and refused.

"I'm not taken' any orders from a Dawg!" insisted Duponte.

"Well he does out rank you, so get to it, Private 1st Class!" chuckled the Captain.

Duponte snarled at Superman as he left the office to get a bucket and mop, and Superman tipped his head and panted joyfully.

When Duponte finally returned with the bucket and mop, the Captain's phone loudly rang, breaking the silence in the Captain's office.

When the Captain answered it, there was a police officer on the other end.

"Captain Landry, this is Detective St. Pierre. There was an incident that took place a few minutes ago and I'd like you to come immediately to the scene," requested the detective.

"What's dis about?" inquired the Captain.

"I can't say over the phone, I'll fill you in on all the details when you get here. The address is 2424 Decatur street, New Orleans…Please come right away," stated the detective.

"Okay, I'm leavin' right now!" exclaimed the Captain and he curiously hung up the phone.

"Never mind dat bucket and mop, Tunder. We got to get over to New Orleans. The Po Po wants to talk to me about somethin' urgent. Go get a truck and get a move on it!

"What about Lunch?!" exclaimed Duponte.

"We'll catch us somethin' after we done der, now Chey Chey, go get a Humvee!" shouted the Captain.

Duponte quickly left and returned several minutes later with a Humvee which had a large machine gun mounted to a turret on top of the Humvee's roof.

The Captain charged out of his office building and froze when he saw the vehicle.

"What sort of Cou-yah are you boy?! Go get a Humvee wid out a 50 caliber Ma-deuce mounted on it!" exclaimed the Captain.

"But Daaad, it's all the motor pool had, and the Sarg told me to take it or leave it. I knew you were in a hurry, so I took it!" replied Duponte

The Captain shrugged his shoulders and shook his head, then called Superman and they all got into the Humvee.

"By da way, don't call me Daaad at the base," stated the Captain.

Chapter 32

The two men quickly left the base, and while preparing to enter the highway ramp, out of nowhere they were recklessly cut off by an old blue haired, stone-faced woman driving a brown minivan who was approaching from the opposite direction!

It caused Duponte to quickly turn off the road, and they crashed over the curb, nearly hitting a utility pole.

When Duponte beeped his horn at the old woman, she cursed crude obscenities at them, raised her hand, threw them an obscene finger gesture, and sped away onto the highway ramp!

"Did you see dat!!!" shouted the Captain.

"That's some crude old granny!" chuckled Duponte.

Captain Landry became en-roadraged and quickly unbuckled his seat belt, and ordered Duponte to chase after her, as he left his seat and positioned himself into the machine gun turret!

"Go after her!! I'm gonna teach dat old Crawfish a lesson! Dis is what's gonna happen to you when you throw a finger at da US Army!" exclaimed the Captain.

Duponte quickly backed up the Humvee and then accelerated onto the highway ramp, and quickly caught up to the crotchety old woman!

Duponte aggressively pulled up next to her, and to his astonishment she glanced over and shouted more crude obscenities at them, and then followed up with the obscene finger gesture again, but this time with both hands!

The Captain was outraged and out of his mind when he saw that, and his Cajun temper had gotten the better of him!

"Pull up in front of that old Crow! I want her to see what's comin!!" shouted the Captain.

Duponte obeyed his order, and accelerated past her and then cut off the old Hag!

The Captain then spun the armored machine gun turret and aimed the massive machine gun directly at the nasty old crows vehicle!

She continued on with even more verbal abuse and harsh hand gestures, disregarding the fact that there was a 50 caliber machine gun now aimed at her!

Finally the Captain couldn't contain himself anymore, and he pulled the trigger!!

The gun cranked out a rip of about 50 automatic rounds directly into the minivan!

It suddenly exploded and blasted itself up more than 50 feet up into the air, flipping over several times before its demolished body came crashing down onto the pavement upside down, and then rolled over several more times before it came to rest in the middle of the highway!

"Baza Grah!!! That'll fix you, you old Sour Son of a Witch!!" shouted the Captain.

****

Seconds later the Captain felt a hand shaking his shoulder….

"Dad, Dad! Snap out of it, we're almost der. You looked like you were having some sort of crazy day dream or somethin'," exclaimed Duponte.

"Where's dat old Hag!" shouted the Captain as he shook off his imaginary altercation with the old Bat.

"Long gone, Captain. She turned off on da ramp to go North and we were goin' South, " stated Duponte.

"Man, she's lucky I ain't prone to road rage. Otherwise I might have been tempted to get into da turret and release da fury of dat Ma-deuce on her," calmly stated the Captain as he closed his eyes,

crossed his arms and smiled as he revisited his day
dream.

Chapter 33

It wasn't an extraordinary day at the Crawdad Shack as the restaurant was filled with its lunch time patrons.

Most of which were sitting at the restaurants counter, slurping down dozens of red boiled crayfish and drinking Cajun lemonade.

The end post stool remained empty, for everyone knew "It was Brud's seat", and if he came along and you were sitting on it, you would be in serious trouble.

Millard was busily serving up buckets as his screen door continually opened and then slamed closed during the lunchtime rush. No one really noticed who was coming and going until Brud suddenly came strolling in with the same young teenage girl still being dragged around by his leash.

Millard looked over his shoulder and sighed with regret as Brud took his place at the end stool, and ordered the girl to "sit" next to him on the floor.

"I see you still have your "puppy" Brud, don't you think it's time to let her go home?" Millard pleaded.

"Shut up and set me up wid a bucket full, and mind your business!" Brud shouted.

Millard threw up his hands and returned to the kitchen when the screen door opened, and a young boy cautiously walked into the restaurant and waited for Millard to appear.

The boy nervously handed Millard a sealed envelope, and asked him if he could give it to Brud.

"Why don't you give it to him yourself? He's sittin' right over there," stated Millard.

The young boy was deathly afraid of Brud, fearing he could also be put on a leash, and he quickly turned and ran out of the restaurant.

Millard seemed confused, and shook the envelope.

He noticed there was a small soft object inside, and it had a slight pungent fragrance to it.

He brought over Brud's order of crawdads, and handed him the envelope.

"What's this?" he gruffed.

"Some kid walked in and asked me to give this to you. Maybe it's something valuable!" chuckled Millard.

Brud took the envelope and looked down at the girl who was nervously sitting on the floor next to him.

"Do you know anything about this?" he questioned.

She shrugged her shoulders, and begged him once again to let her go home.

He harshly snapped the leash and she fell over on the filthy restaurant floor, and she began to cry.

Millard was flabbergasted and once again asked him to let the girl go home.

"Brud, I'll pay you! How much do you want to let the child go home?" inquired Millard.

"Back off Millard, or you are gonna have a bad rest of your day. Now get out of my face so I can enjoy my crawdads!" he shouted, and revealed his gun holstered under his jacket.

Millard reluctantly walked away as Brud began opening the envelope that Millard had given to him.

As Brud opened it, he was surprised to see a lucky rabbit's foot stuffed in the envelope.

"Hey look Millard, someone sent me a lucky rabbit's foot!" shouted Brud.

He glanced down at the girl and thought for a moment about giving it to her.

"You want this to chew on little puppy?" he dangled and tempted her with the furry object.

As she slowly reached for it, he quickly snapped it away, and tucked it into his shirt pocket and began eating his lunch.

"I don't see how that rabbit was so lucky if his foot got snatched off and is now in your pocket, Brud," stated Millard.

Suddenly there was a rutkis outside of the restaurant, and dozens of people began screaming, and running away in all directions!

"Get out of the way!! There's a mad dog on the loose!!" shouted a man.

The loud growling and wheezing of a mad dog could be heard approaching rapidly, and racing toward the restaurant!

It was getting louder and louder, as the raging dog got closer and closer!

Suddenly it vaulted itself up into the air, and came crashing through the screen door of the Crawdad Shack, and went directly at Brud!!

Everyone inside the restaurant hastily evacuated the restaurant, including the young girl on the leash, as the dog viciously attacked Brud!!

Chapter 34

Captain Landry and Duponte had just arrived at the address the detective had given him, and was surprised to discover that it was "The Crawdad Shack"!

The police were still taking statements from the witnesses, as the coroner was just loading a large bloodied body bag into their vehicle.

Millard noticed Duponte and he came rushing over!

"A wild dog blasted through my screen door and killed Brud! I have never seen a dog go at someone like that before! It was like the dawg was locked on and targeted Brud, and it ripped him to bloody pieces!" exclaimed Millard.

The Captain and Duponte looked at each other, and believed that the dog could have been implanted with the "Tiger Shark".

"What happened to da dawg?" inquired the Captain.

"He just stopped after Brud was dead, and it turned around, wagged his tail and ran out the way he came in, and then disappeared!

Animal control is out looking for it!" exclaimed Millard.

"Did you notice anything unusual about Brud? Did he have a wet stain on his jacket dat might have smelled odd?" inquired Duponte.

"No, but a kid came in with an envelope and asked me to give it to Brud. It was a lucky rabbit's foot and it had a funny smell to it. Brud put it into his pocket after he opened it. I guess it wasn't so lucky for Brud. Not that we're gonna miss him," replied Millard.

A detective wandered over and introduced himself as Detective St. Pierre.

"Thanks, for coming so quickly, Captain. I was at the incident at Fort Chips, where a Lieutenant was attacked and killed by a vicious dog. We are wondering if this incident might tie in together with that one, and maybe this might be the same wild dog on the loose?" stated the detective.

The Captain glanced over at Duponte and discreetly motioned to him to keep his mouth shut.

"Well, I'm not so sure dese two incidences do tie in. No one really knew what happened wid da Lieutenant since da perpetrator disappeared. For all we knew, it could have been a coyote or a rabid raccoon," replied the Captain.

The detective listened and agreed.

"Sorry to drag you down here. If you think of anything, please let me know," and the detective handed him his contact card.

"Will do," replied the Captain.

The detective walked away and joined another group of detectives as they tried to sort out the crime scene.

"Holy Trinity! Koz is alive!" whispered Duponte.

"How do you know it was Kozlowski?" inquired the Captain.

"We came here after we picked up da dawgs from Duffy. I wanted to show him a good time while we were in New Orleans, and he got pretty upset when he saw Brud come strutten in wid a young girl he had put on a leash. He wanted to do somethin' about it, but I stopped him," stated Duponte.

"We've got to find him before he takes off. He must still be around here someplace," stated the Captain.

The two men quickly returned back to the Humvee.

"Can't say Koz put da Tiger Shark to bad use," stated Duponte.

"We can't let an Awol vigilante out wid something dat dangerous! We have to find him and get it back!" stated the Captain.

"Laissez les bon temps Roulez'," stated Duponte.

"Chey Chey...Let's go find him!" replied his father.

And they quickly drove off.

"Hey wait! We forgot to get a bucket of crawdads!" exclaimed Duponte.

"Never mind, Kozlowski has to be somewhere around here, lets go check the freight yard, it's close by!" stated the Captain.

Chapter 35

The blaring horns of a huge diesel powered freight trains engine blasted, as the 200 car train slowly began rolling out of the New Orleans freight yard.

Inside one of the open boxcars a mysterious man wearing a brightly colored floral Hawaiian shirt and a small brimmed fedora hat, which hung low over his forehead, sat against the wall of the rumbling boxcar as it left the freight yard.

He sat there holding a steel Attache' case, and while staring out the open doorway, he watched his life pass behind him.

Bearing witness to murders, thugs and child abusers all his life in New York City didn't sit well with him, and so he decided that maybe, just maybe he could do something about it.

If nothing else to try to make the world a better place.

He continued staring out the open doorway when he noticed a military Humvee with a machine gun turret pass by the moving train on a parallel road, heading towards the freight yard that he had just left.

He thought he noticed Duponte driving the vehicle and the Captain in the passenger seat.

"They must now know I'm alive and using the Tiger Shark. The cops must have notified them after I turned it on Brud," he thought.

He knew that his life had completely changed and now he was on the run.

"They'll be looking for me, and they'll try to stop me from doing society a favor, and eliminating the scourge of the earth. If they can catch me," he whispered to himself.

Laissez les bon temps roulez'

About the Author

Coming soon!

Another exciting story by B.L. Blocher

As the Sparrows Fly

Growing up on a dairy farm in Binghamton NY in the 1950's was not easy, especially when you had an older brother like Lenny living under the same roof as you. Lenny gives a new twisted dimension to sibling rivalry as he reeks havoc on his family and then later joins up with the Chicago mob where he can continue on with his degenerative violent behavior.

If you thought Wolfie was bad, wait till you get a load of Lenny in this action packed thriller!

Books available now by B.L. Blocher:

The WATCHMAKER
The SILVER ORCHID
RAZZLE DAZZLE

Coming soon: *AS THE SPARROWS FLY*

and

THE WATCHMAKER PART II "THE CHOSEN"

E-Mail Thewatchmaker1939@gmail.com